D0049081

BUT THEN I CAME BACK

BUT THEN I CAME BACK

ESTELLE LAURE

Houghton Mifflin Harcourt
Boston New York

Copyright © 2017 by Estelle Laure

www.hmhco.com

The text was set in Norlik.

Library of Congress Cataloging-in-Publication Data
Names: Laure, Estelle, author.
Title: But then I came back / Estelle Laure.
Description: Boston; New York: Houghton Mifflin Harcourt, [2017].
Summary: After a month in a coma, eighteen-year-old Eden finds it hard to resume her life and relationships but forms an unlikely connection with Joe, who visits his best friend, Jaz, another coma patient, every day.
Identifiers: LCCN 2016029372 | ISBN 9780544531260 (hardback)
Subjects: | CYAC: Coma—Fiction. | Interpersonal relations—Fiction. | Family life—Fiction. | Supernatural—Fiction.
Classification: LCC PZ7.1.L38 But 2017 | DDC [Fic]—dc23
LC record available at https://lccn.loc.gov/2016029372

Manufactured in the United States of America
DOC 10 9 8 7 6 5 4 3 2 1
4500645358

For Chris—With you,
I am awake.

A solitude ten thousand fathoms deep
Sustains the bed on which we lie, my dear:
Although I love you, you will have to leap;
Our dream of safety has to disappear.

—W. H. Auden

BEFORE

(november)

YOU BLAME THE INTERNET FOR THE WHOLE THING.

Your mom made tequila-lime pie for dessert. You didn't have any because dessert always tastes like too much, but you did pilfer the bottle of Patrón Silver she used and sneak it to the river. You needed it because you had to walk down the hill in the middle of the night and your leather jacket wasn't warm enough for early November, but you were stubborn and stupid and wouldn't wear a puffer coat because gross. You didn't wear snow gear, either. Not even your combat boots, idiot. You wore flats. Flats in this weather, Eden. But you also took the tequila because, aside from an awkward exchange at Fred's Restaurant where Lucille works, you hadn't talked to her in six weeks and you figured, why not bring a little help for the both of you? Still, you don't blame the tequila for what's happening now.

You blame the Internet. It informed you, on a site it tricked you into, that there was going to be an epic once-in-five-years supermoon and that the universe was demanding you change your ways.

Move or be moved, it said. It was like a storm watch for the soul. You could practically hear the voice, see the guy standing in front of the monitor in some bad suit, waving his arms about in warning.

Fatepocalypse is coming in from the southwesterly direction at roughly eighty miles per hour, you imagine him saying in his uptight voice. *Citizens should be on the lookout. It's headed straight for all of us, but I'm especially talking to Eden Jones. Oh boy, oh buddy, this one is coming for you, girl. Safety Department recommends you cease carrying on like a human and stay indoors. Preferably forever.*

If you were naive enough to believe in a universe that communicates with humans (which you are not), one that you might, in fact, be able to have a conversation with (which you cannot), you would demand to know why it speaks in staticky gibberish made up of planets and symbols and expects people to understand it.

At first you blew off the Internet's warning because astrology is ridiculous nonsense, but then the whole week was such a suckfest, you began to wonder. It was so bad that you got paranoid about that moon, and ever more pissed off at the Internet, because brains are so powerful, just the fact that you read the warning could have made it true. But when Lucille texted you telling you she needed you, you thought maybe if you went, things would go back to their regularly scheduled pleasant level of suck instead of this extreme. Secretly, even secretly from yourself, you thought you might appease the nonexistent, confusing entity that was having its fun toying with you, by showing up for Lucille after, admittedly, being kind of a bitch to her when she needed you most.

You never meant to be horrible to her. You have long claimed that the only thing you really hate is mean girls, and you wouldn't be one on purpose. But ever since Lucille decided your newly philandering, almost engaged twin brother is her soul mate, being around her has gotten really hard to do without violent impulses. Every time Digby moped all over you about her and loving her *and* Elaine, and his deep, angsty struggles between right and wrong, and *what should he do,* you wanted to shake Lucille by the shoulder until her head jiggled free of her neck socket.

Because first of all, if a girl has any ambition, she shouldn't be a pawn in someone else's drama, much less be the cause of it. Second, cheating is sordid and cheap. And third, it is a conflict of interest that isn't actually all that interesting but is all anybody can talk about. At first the entire seamy debacle (because it is a debacle) was something to watch, but after a while, it seemed to you that it was nothing but pathetic.

So the bad moon rising is how you found yourself on your rock tonight, the flat one at the river's edge that you used to pretend into a throne when you were little. You still do, because you fancy yourself a queen and the river your queendom. This bend of the river, flanked by rocks and ancient trees and an old train car, is your private place. The willows are all stripped down this time of year, except for the sheen of icicle glass. You like willows best of all the trees, because they know how to bow to a lady, but also because if you cut them deep, they cry.

Lucille was crying, sitting under them looking like a giant snowball in her winter jacket and hat, and the ice in you was melting as she shifted around, chewing on her lip, her nails, her nail beds, crossing her legs then uncrossing them, moving, always moving, apologizing for her flaws with every twitch.

Heart-in-her-hand girl.

You were glad to have come so you could remind yourself all about your mad, passionate love for her, which had hurt so much to try to forget, but you were distracted, too. Your whirlpool mind wouldn't stop circling the drain, whirring on and on about your stupid, average, small-town New Jersey mediocrity, that your future was now nothing but an endless, murky path. Your third cigarette in a row wasn't doing any good either. It spilled through your lungs. They ached, and your head, your

4

stomach too, and you knew you should—but you couldn't—stop chain smoking.

"I'm really sorry about the ballet thing." Lucille's voice glued you to the rock just as you were about to stand, to tell her you were going home. "You should keep on," she said.

"I will." You tried not to think about the lady in New York with the deer bones bending toward you, whispering nightmares about your future low into your ear. "Just now I know it's not going to do me any good. Denial is for losers." You said this out loud, because Lucille needed to hear it as much as you did. "Face your crap and move on. Otherwise you'll get old and depressed and turn into a scary pod person whose most pressing issue in life is when they get to trade in the can of Dr Pepper for the can of Bud. It's true." You took one last drag of your smoke. "Look around."

Lucille tittered, but that easy-chair reality wasn't funny. It was entirely possible. Probable, even. People settle down in front of the idiot box and never get up again because it requires too much effort. Sometimes, though you would never speak it, you think it would be a hell of a lot easier to want a simple life. You long for a recliner, and for a dull, compliant mind, instead of the one you got, which is a lot more flailing octopus than floating manatee.

You crushed your smoke and stood high on your toes. You

5

stretched, reached your arms toward the sky, and asked the moon if it was satisfied now, if you had done enough to turn things around and avoid the storm by being here, by paying respects, by cleaning up your friendship with Lucille.

That was it . . . the moment it happened.

Your feet lost their grip like an answer.

You teetered on ice, tried to steady yourself. It was too fast.

You wanted to call out to Lucille for help, but before you could, a thud that was your own head. A bright jangle. Pain. You tried to fight. You couldn't. You were already in the water.

You waited to go unconscious, but you didn't. At least, you think you didn't. Rocks battered your legs, and water slipped into your lungs, heavier than the smoke but just as achy.

This was a crisis, and you knew it in your flailing octopus brain, but it didn't touch you. Because you weren't you anymore. You were nowhere near yourself. Not in any way. You weren't even human. No, girl. You were the wind whipping at the pages of a book; you were a grass ocean, swaying. You were the willow, weeping, weeping, and you hum-hummed every lullaby all at once, and it was soft and beautiful and infinite.

And the cradle will fall.

And down will come—

Hey, pay attention!

I'm telling you this so you'll remember.

Because you're weightless now, and you have to remember this so you don't forget who you are.

Eden Jones. Eden Austen Jones. Age seventeen. Daughter to John and Jane Jones. Twin sister to Digby Riley Jones. Best friend to Lucille Bennett. You live in Cherryville, New Jersey, in the brand-new subdivision on the top of the hill, in your parents' dream house. You handpicked the carpet in your room, the paint on your wall. You are a ballerina. You collect quotes from books by people wiser than you, mostly dead. You write down those quotes and repeat them aloud to yourself until they are embossed on your soul. You dream of fame. What's in a name a rose by any other name would smell as sweet it means nothing nothing and everything and youdon'tcareyoudon'tmin ditatallnotonebit.

Which is why you let go.

It's so damn sweet to be nothing but a riversong.

Patient name: Eden Jones

Glasgow Coma Scale Test

Eye Opening Response: None (1)

Best Verbal Response: None (1)

Best Motor Response: None (1)

Total score: 3

Prognosis: Poor

LUCILLE AND I ARE DOWN TO SKIVVIES.

It's June, and the water is chilly. I keep myself mostly under to the neck even though it's just me and Lucille, because Mom still buys me underpants from the girl section, so I'm in a white bralette and underwear with butterflies on it.

I'm thirteen, Mother, I tell her all the time.

Woman. Doesn't. Listen.

Lucille has a real bra that clasps in the back instead of going over her head. And it's pink. It even has lace, because her mom cares about her as a person. Lucille also has flesh and fat to put into her bra while I'm more like a human hanger. Her underwear is black and rides high on her hips. She looks dangerous and like she might accidentally knock someone unconscious with the flick of a curve. *Boom. Gotcha.* When we took our clothes off to get in the river today, we both tried to cover up with our hands. My stomach boiled when we did that.

I can't see Lucille, but I feel her next to me, bobbling around.

8

That's not accurate. She doesn't actually bobble. She glides, slices through the water, knifelike. She moved here to New Jersey from Los Angeles when we were little, and she says before her aunt died and her parents got the house next to mine, she spent all the time at the beach, surfing with her dad. But whatever she did in LA, we're not the same. The water and me, we dance.

We have to keep to the eddies mostly, because my mom is so ugh. *Controlling,* Dad says, and she claims that we'll drown if we go too far, if we let the current take us. *Might as well be a riptide.* We thought she was bluffing about following us, but after she stalked us like a creepy creeper a few times, we stopped going too far out and she left us alone. Finally.

Even so, I like to get to a place in the river where my feet don't touch down, so I can practice my ballet without pushing on bruises and blisters. I don't complain about them out loud because they're part of being a dancer, but that doesn't mean they don't hurt.

First position, second, third.

A person needs to be efficient with said person's time, and someday I'm going to be the most famous ballerina who has ever lived. People will be all, *Anna Pavlova? Mikhail Baryshnikov? Nobodies! Now, Eden Jones, that is someone worth paying attention to.*

Mom and Dad tell Digby and me that efficiency and

consistency are the keys to results. In sports, business, *and* brushing teeth. I run my tongue across my braces and turn my face to the sun so it scalds my cheeks tight. I like how they hurt. It takes me exactly five seconds to get roasted because of my skin, so there's no point in fighting it unless I'm going to spend my summer in a muumuu like the one Gran wears all the time.

Fry me.

Lucille splashes me, and it tingles like fairy dust.

I started swearing recently. I like it very much, so I practice now on Lucille, taste the hard consonants, the hissing *s*, the brick of the *ck*. And then I chase her.

She gets me by the leg and yanks. I raise my hands, not to keep from going all the way underwater, but because we should be as graceful in life as we are on stage, in practice, in every moment. Madame says so.

I submerge.

Submerge. I love that word.

In seventh-grade biology, we learned about eyes. Kind of ruined them for me, and so I've been looking at them in pieces. I can't help myself. I don't know whether they're the window to the soul like people claim, but they say something important. With Lucille and me treading water, holding hands, I dissect hers into parts, those eyes I know so well.

Irises: blue

Pupils: dilated

Eyelashes: long and dark

Eyelids: full

Sclera: chalk white

More . . .

Skin: tan

Hair: blond

Lips: modelish (annoying)

Legs: long

Boobs: present and accounted for

Arches: superior

Lucille: best friend

She shakes her head back and forth, and her hair spreads into a seaweed halo.

But something is wrong.

We've been under the water for a long time, and Lucille is changing.

Her face is both elongating and getting smaller. Her hair falls off her head and floats away. These are not Lucille's eyes.

Irises: green and brown with blue around the edges

Pupils: dilating madly

Eyelashes: short and black

Eyelids: thick

Sclera: almost disappeared

Skin: brown

Hair: barely a stubble

Lips: thin on top

Legs: muscular

Boobs: not much happening there

Arches: none

Name: unknown

The girl who is not Lucille who has tattoos of angels on her arms opens her mouth like she's trying to tell me something. Bubbles drift toward the surface. That's where I want to be. I kick my legs, but she tugs me back and forces my wrist.

She won't let me go.

A flower blooms from her lips. It's black, a water creature, and it swims away.

I want to go up. Up. Out.

I wriggle free, look back at her. The farther up I go, the more she sinks. I break through the surface, punch into night, into my longer body, and I land in my room.

Now.

I know it's now instead of then because of the posters on the wall and the pairs of ballet slippers lined up from when I was eight to the ones I got last year. I also know because my book still rests on my bedside table. My journal is still on the corner of my desk. The pictures of Lucille and me on my board. Inside the desk will be a box filled with quotes, blank journals I buy and swear to fill up, and performance pictures I never look at that are shoved to the back. Pieces of me.

I want to get into bed, under my cozy blankets, and sleep this away.

But there's no room because Digby and Lucille are there, their heads a mayhem of blond and red. I jump in between them to pry them apart and wake them, but I sweep right through and wind up in a heap on the floor. I do it again and again. There's a gelatinous ripple as I slam against them, but in the end, they remain asleep.

Am I a ghost?

That would be so cool. I guess it would be sad, too, but I would make an excellent haunter. I would mess people up.

It's important to deal with reality, but in order to do that, a person has to know what reality is. A person has to know, for instance, if she's even a person at all, so I try again, though I'm getting bored by the whole thing. I scream in their faces, I jump on the bed. I assess, looking about for signs of the afterlife, of other ghostlike entities. I half expect to find Gran on my window seat, smoking a cigarette, telling me between puffs that it's time to go with her into the light.

There's no light. There's no Gran, either. Just this half version of me, and Digby and Lucille.

I perch on my footboard, rest my head in my hands. I'm not tired or hungry. I'm not even mad. I'm not anything at all. I wish I had my phone.

My brother's mouth hangs open, and he snores with every third breath. After I've been watching the two of them for so long that several civilizations have both risen and fallen and I'm about to try to figure out how to get all the way dead, Lucille comes awake like she's swimming toward consciousness from a great distance, her sandy hair in a bun, her cheeks mashed and lined with pillow burns, eyes half open and effortful. She smiles at me lazily, sleep still on her.

I approach her slowly, not wanting to frighten her, not sure she can see me. I want to ask her if I'm dead. I get close and try to hug her, but I slip through her and the wall and then, before I can think, before I have time to adjust, I'm with my mother like the getting to Lucille passed me by.

Mom is fully clothed, face-down on her foam mattress, on her taupe cotton sheets. I think she's asleep, but then she mewls into her pillow, a high-pitched whine. She cries my name. There's a picture of me in her right hand in a frame I made for her, a badly painted pale green wooden thing. In it, I have pigtails, freckles, a bright, uneven smile, and my teeth are an unholy wreck. When you're a mom, you probably get sad for every version of your kid when they're gone, for every day you got with them and every day you'll never have.

So I must be dead.

I don't know how to feel about this, but I do know I don't like to see my mom so destroyed by my absence. I fold myself around my mother's slender, hard body, cocoon her there. But when I ask myself if it's a bad thing to be dead, even with her furrowed in my arms, there is only one answer.

No.

Mom trembles violently, like she heard my thoughts, like she's being hit with a defibrillator, again and again, and she makes animal noises, grips the pillow with a fist. She's flat-lining.

I blink.

Stillness.

I'm nowhere, in blank space, surrounded by white.

An inky, velvet bud sprouts from the lines in the palm of my pale hand. As it unfurls, its onyx petals undulate and a sticky yellow bubbles in dewdrops from its center and floats in front of me, as if there is no gravity and nothing to bind it.

Voices weave around me, ones I recognize. I single out the

15

sounds of Reggie, one of my best friends my whole life. He tells me about bathing suits, about how to choose the perfect one. I should not attempt the Brazilian cheeky, he says, with my shamefully flat behind. Then I'm remembering when we were five and I sobbed because we weren't in the same kindergarten class and so did Reggie, and we both gave our parents such a hard time that the school actually switched us.

A petal falls from the flower and floats up, as does a trace of panic.

My mother's voice, low and tremulous.

"But I love your feet only because they walked upon the earth and upon the wind and upon the waters, until they found me."

Pablo Neruda.

I lose three more petals.

I'm chaotically worried. An entire lifetime of memories with my mom is in front of me, and I can't ignore them.

The Eden Jones of me zips and buckles like a straitjacket as the rest of the flower floats from my palm and disappears.

Finally, my Lucille speaks. She is not shaky. "Wake up, Eden," she says. "You are going to wake up."

AND I DO.

Beeps.

Tubes everywhere. They slither from my throat, out of my stomach. They pump and bleat. Something plastic or rubber is in my nose, and more of the same burrows into the skin at my throat like a parasitic slug.

I'm pinned by a matrix of machines. People dressed in pale blue dash and duck around me as I thrash. I can't stop. There is so much noise, clattering and screeching everywhere.

"Oh my God," I hear a woman's voice say. "Dear lord in heaven, she's awake! I knew it. I knew she would come back!" She is laughing. And also maybe crying. "Out of my way," she says. "Make room."

"Eden?" It's Digby. "Eden! Eden, Eden, Eden!" He might be crying, too. "Are you," he says. "Are you really . . ."

I want this off of me, all of it, out of me. I'm an inside-out pair of socks, twisted around myself, all my innards on display.

17

I want to tell them not to touch me, to get away, but when I open my mouth, nothing comes out.

"Stop it," one of the Blues says, the same voice that was yelling and praising before. "Stop it now, Eden Jones." She said my name. She knows who I am. Her voice is sure, no nonsense. "You are going to hurt yourself if you don't stop that right now. You've got to keep your medicine and food in place until you're stable and until it can all be properly removed." She readjusts tubes that pinch and poke. I kick like a baby, resist even though I already know I shouldn't, that it won't do any good. I want to bite something, anything, everything.

The Blue comes in close, places one of my cheeks in each of her hands, and makes thorough eye contact with me, so I can see her black eyeliner and her carefully pinked lips. "I know this is disorienting and scary, baby, but you need to relax. You survived." She releases my cheeks. "You already did that. Now, relax, like I said. Relax. We've got you."

I touch the tube at my throat.

"Don't try to talk for now. Your body needs some time to remember its job. It forgot, baby." She smiles, and I see that she's kind, and so pretty. I go limp.

"Edes." Digby's voice again. My twin. Green eyes outshine the Blue, and behind him, Lucille, who takes one of my hands in hers.

"Stay," the Blue says, like I'm a naughty puppy. "You got people here. Lucky girl." The Blue releases me, and I lie still, and when she's certain I'm not going to flop around anymore, she backs away, eyes on me as if I will pounce if left unchecked.

"You're okay." It's a question and an answer. Digby threads his fingers into my free hand. "Well," he says, "ish. I mean, now you're okay. There was an accident." His mouth snaps shut, then hangs open. He looks like a fish. When I smile, my lips crack and burn like someone took a razor to them. I roll fetal. Need water.

Water.

There was water, the river, the swimming, my room, my mom, the flowers. I've lost something. There's water now, here, salting my skin. It leaks down my temples, into my hair.

Digby scans around me as though for help. The Blue gives him a nod I don't miss, then fusses with tubes and bags and buttons some more.

"Edes." Digby speaks deliberately. "Listen to me. You were in a coma."

The ceiling is broken into squares, and those squares are broken into squares, and on and on like that.

"You've been gone for a month. Do you understand what I'm saying?"

I nod. But a month how? And where? That place In Between

the water and here was forty-five minutes, an hour maybe, a day at most. Wasn't it? My head thuds on a pillow. There's bald skin on the cotton.

"They drilled into your skull to relieve pressure on your brain when you first came in," he says. "You hit your head. That's why they shaved you. It's fine. Nothing permanent."

And if you squint the right way, you can make the squares on the ceiling pirouette.

"Aw, Edes," Digby says. "Don't worry, you're still ugly."

Lucille smacks him.

The Blue gives him a look, blocks my view of him, wipes at the sides of my eyes and across my forehead with something cool. She shushes and tuts and then introduces herself as Rita.

"Open your mouth a bit, honey." She rubs ice chips over my lips, against my dry tongue and the insides of my cheeks. Never on the earth has there been anything as awesome and right as that cool.

"Eden." Digby trails his finger along the inside of his sleeve, a thing he only does when he's stressed. "Do you get what I'm saying? That you've been in a coma?"

I nod again, and swallow. My throat doesn't want to cooperate.

"God." He flops his head between his arms. "I don't know how to do this."

Lucille strokes my arm in small circles. There's so much pain. Mostly on the inside.

"They said you're going to stay awake this time." Lucille sniffles. "That's great, right? It's like a miracle."

Yeah, it's great.

"Because you blinked three weeks ago, and we thought you were waking up and then you didn't," Digby says. "It messed us all up pretty bad."

"You fell," Lucille says. "You remember? You slipped. At the spot. I couldn't get you. It was so fast. I'm sorry."

"Lucille saved you," Digby says. "I mean, she ran into the river and pulled you out. Otherwise . . ."

He brushes a strip of fallen hair behind Lucille's ears. She blushes so hard the ear he swiped turns racecar, valentine, flapper-dress red.

"I told you," she says to him, "stop saying that. I'm the reason she was there—"

He kisses her silent, quickly, but it's enough to tell me I didn't imagine that In Between place or the two of them in my bed. That was real. As real as this hospital, these horrible bright lights, this awful pink blanket.

Lucille's half of the best-friends necklace we got when we were ten glows against her chest, her silver hoop earrings, her dusty blue eyes, and Digby with his hair like mine, his black hoodie, the green T-shirt underneath, the green and black striped beanie on his head. They are all the good colors.

I ache down my arms and legs, my neck. Only my feet don't hurt. I rub them against each other. No blisters, no bruises. They're smooth and soft.

I throw the covers off and sit up, and I'm immediately so dizzy I swoon back onto my pillow.

"Uh-uh," Rita says as she tucks the blanket around me, bug-in-a-rug style. I do not feel snug as a bug. I feel tied and bound, restrained. "Nobody's passing out on my watch, so you stay put." She gives me such a solid stare I start to wonder about her life. Does she have kids? She looks like she could be in school with me. Young. At last she says, "You're going to have to do one thing at a time. You lost fifteen pounds you didn't have to spare, and you haven't walked or talked in a month, plus you got a nasty concussion. So you calm down."

I want to go back to the place with the flower, where there was nothing. Not a worry. Not a care. Not a human body and a life to manage and all these people.

"The docs are on their way," she says. "Don't you worry."

I want my mom. I want my mom.

"Mom's coming now," Digby says, like he heard me. "She and Dad went to have dinner late." He fumbles with his hat.

"It's the first time one of them hasn't been here since your accident." This is an apology. "It figures," he says.

My heartbeat slows and thumps grudgingly against my rib cage.

I took a deep breath and listened to the old brag of my heart.

I am, I am, I am.

Sylvia Plath.

The dull thud bumps through my chest, up my neck, and lodges itself behind my eyes.

Yes, I am. I'm back on this earth, a measly human. You know how I know that?

Because nothing besides life hurts this much.

I don't want to force my eyes to stay open anymore. They're too heavy.

And so I close them.

Patient name: Eden Jones

Glasgow Coma Scale Test

Eye Opening Response: To speech (2)

Best Verbal Response: Inappropriate words (3)

Best Motor Response: Abnormal flexion (3)

Total Score: 8

Prognosis: Undetermined

THE SINKING GIRL IS IN THE ROOM DOWN THE HALL FROM MINE.

It took me a minute to recognize her out of context. Bald head. Angel tattoos. That's when I knew for sure it was her. We are the only two coma girls. The rest of this section of the hospital is made up of a few really old people in wheelchairs. Strokes, mostly, faces slack, sometimes drooling. This hospital is so small there's no pediatric section, not for neurology, so we're all squished in together.

Not her, though. She's like Snow White in her coffin. Preserved behind a pane of glass. Smooth. Since I don't know her name, I've dubbed her Vasquez. *Aliens* is almost my favorite movie, and Vasquez is the best character in it. She's this machine-gun-wielding badass, the only woman besides Ripley, and she kills it. She isn't afraid of acidic monstrosities. She isn't afraid of anything.

My Vasquez has black hair that's growing in a fuzzy stubble on a really nicely shaped oval head. Not everyone should try to pull off being baldish, but it looks good on her. She also has about a billion stitches across her forehead, but her skin is otherwise a dusty brown, except for where the wings from her tattoos peek out from under her hospital gown sleeves.

To be clear, I don't think this girl is actually Vasquez. My brain is reaching for anything to entertain. I'm not allowed to watch TV yet, or have a computer, or even a phone. I need time, they say. An unstimulating environment. Until I'm right again. Until I'm not confused anymore.

I don't remember all that much about the confusion. Only that it was kind of like a high-speed nightmare, and they tell me it lasted about a week. At one point I thought my parents were secretly CIA agents and that they were in the hospital to kill me. I remember flashes of memories, too. Almost choking on spinach soup when I was two, falling down the stairs, accidentally breaking a Christmas ball in my hand. Bad memories from when I was really little, I don't know why. I find it kind of entertaining now, but it was scary when it was happening, like a computer running through random files as it reboots. I think I'm back to normal now.

Yesterday when I went by Vasquez's room (and by "went," I mean old-lady shuffled with my walker), there was a boy sitting in the chair at her bedside. Shaggy, glossy black hair, a green and red flannel shirt plus some baggy jeans and work boots, solid sinewy forearms. That's all I could see without flattening my face against the window like a psycho. I wanted to.

I named him Hudson, after Vasquez's sidekick. I imagine the two of them in headbands, sweating, fighting it out to the death with an alien they can't win against because it lives inside of them. Maybe the alien gestated in Vasquez's brain. Maybe that's why the stitches, why the coma. Facesuckers. It's plausible.

Obviously, I'm making all this up about Vasquez's personality, about Hudson being her sidekick buddy with ambivalent secret romantic tension. I could be totally wrong about them. She could favor white lace and pick wildflowers in her spare time, enjoy a nice picnic by the lake on a weekend afternoon. Him too. Maybe they dig a pastoral frolic.

But I doubt it.

Spying on Vasquez is both a pragmatic and obvious choice because there are fishbowl windows on all the rooms in the neurointensive care unit so they (we) can be easily observed.

"You ready, baby?"

It's Mom.

How long have we been standing here? How long have I been gaping through the window? Time isn't what it was before. I keep missing things.

Mom gives my shoulder a light push and tucks her arm into mine. She doesn't approve of my fascination with Vasquez, I can tell, and I am definitely not going to explain it to her. Every time I pause in front of Vasquez's room, Mom exhales like she's concentrating, with difficulty, on maintaining her patience.

Hudson isn't here today, which is really too bad since it's hard to figure someone out when they aren't present. The chair sits empty at her bedside. Poor Vasquez. All alone.

"Come on," Mom says. "The doctor wants you to practice."

She means I need to work on my walking, but really I need to practice being human again. I seem to have lost my touch.

Bye, Vasquez. I wave and get nothing but beeps in return.

Mom furrows her brow (there has been much brow furrowing).

I tap her arm. Onward. Phlebotomy awaits.

In all this wandering about the hospital from department to department, we've established that

- I am the proud owner of critical illness myopathy, which means I'm tired.
- As well as a concussion, which means I'm cranky.
- And additionally, I have to go for swallow therapy

because of prolonged intubation, which means talking and eating are hard.

- I also have some nerve damage in my legs, which means a slight limp that may or may not be permanent.
- This equals physical therapy.
- Every day.
- And bonus: I am skeleton and skin. I mean that literally. My flesh pulls so tight against my bones that every time I have to get naked to change my clothes, I try to squint myself blind. It's disturbing, even more so since I always wished to be thinner and thinner and lighter and lighter. Only now I realize what's left when all the softness is gone. Not much. It is not much.

We pass a framed picture of a vase, one of a garden, and then hang a left at the daisy, which turns from white to black as we go. I don't freak out and have a violent panic attack because this isn't the first time it's happened with the flowers. Also I'm too tired for violent panic attacks. Maybe some wires got crossed when I came back. Maybe I didn't get all the way online. Because ever since I woke up, I've been seeing the black flowers everywhere, like they're following me.

With a concussion, they tell me, anything is possible. I got a solid whack to the brain. Who knows what could happen when

28

you've got bruised gray matter? But there's a little voice telling me that's not it. It says that I dragged some crazy back from death if those flowers are as real as anything else I can touch or see. Best to ignore that voice, I think. Best to suffocate it to death.

A petal drifts to the floor in front of me. I step on it, then pull the pen from my pocket and scribble.

Book, I write. Then a question mark.

Since I still can't talk much, this three-by-two notebook is all I have.

Mom glances at the paper, then at me, then clutches her very ugly scarf around her neck with her free arm. I made that thing for her when I was trying to be crafty like Lucille. It was immediately apparent that I was not a knitting genius.

"They're in your room, honey," she says. "Your books."

There are a variety of favorites from my shelf at home, stuffed into a purple grocery bag that reads CHERRYVILLE FARM-ERS' MARKET. That bag made me a vicious sort of homesick. It was a fine selection of books, though. Some of my favorite old guys. Steinbeck, a smattering of Faulkner, Cormac McCarthy. And then my ladies. Anne Sexton poetry, Alice Hoffman, Anne Tyler, Patti Smith, and *Song of Solomon* by Toni Morrison, which is a bound sigh trapped on paper. Normally that would be enough to keep me busy, but I haven't been able to get interested.

29

NEAR DEATH EXPERIENCES, I scrawl. All caps. Mom serves me a blank look, so I underline it.

"Why would you want that?" Mom maintains her firm grip on my arm even though we aren't moving now. This is supposed to be so I won't fall, but really, she's the one who might topple. Mom isn't right since I woke up either. She's off. Usually she's wiry and busy and doesn't suffer nonsense. She's made of metal. Or was. But she's twitchy now, like she's constantly jumping to sounds no one else can hear.

"Please," I whisper. I pause to swallow several times. Talking is still like flexing a muscle in a phantom leg.

"You want a book about near-death experiences? Really?"

The hall fills with the smells of coffee and disinfectant that drift toward us from the nurses' station like a slow-moving wave.

I nod.

"Why would you want to read about that? Did something happen?"

I shrug. Mom's an atheist. I am too. Was. I don't know anything anymore, and that's the point. I want to investigate what has happened to other people. People like me.

But I am so not getting into that with her.

My hand goes to my chest.

"You know," Mom says, peering at me, "our brains do all sorts of things when we experience a loss of consciousness the way you did. When the brain is in danger, it fights. You might see images, lights . . ." She trails off.

I'm sure she's right about that. But how do you explain Vasquez? How do you explain that?

"You can talk to me," she says. "I mean, if you experienced anything. You can talk to me about it if you want to."

I shake my head.

"Later, I mean. When you get your voice back," she says. "This is not nothing, Eden. You had a major, major accident. I don't want you to be afraid to say whatever you need to."

I'm not afraid.

She is.

I stroke her cheek with the side of my hand, hoping she'll take the hint and stop prying. I nod toward the end of the hall.

"But"—she hesitates as we continue padding toward the doors—"if you really want a book like that, I'm sure I can find something."

The automatic doors swing open, and Hudson is on the other side, arms stuffed with white flowers. Carnations. They smell like candy. *He* smells like candy, like a dangerous treat. He has eyes like the dirt those flowers were born in. A crooked mouth. Plump lips. Worn hands. Same green and red flannel as yesterday. As he passes, I'm lost in the shock of his face. I don't know what I imagined, but it wasn't this.

He looks at me, too. What does he see? A redhead with bald spots? A freckled, limping freak in a hoodie and drooping black leggings? Did he gaze through my window when I was an almost dead girl, too, instead of one who is almost alive? Did he give me a name?

The doors close behind me with a decided swish.

I GIVE BLOOD.

Mom tells me to choose a focal point and reminds me to breathe through my nose when they prick me, so I don't pass out. The focal point I choose is her drawn face, which looks as flimsy as tissue paper, like you could blow her away with an extra-strong exhale.

"That's right, honey," she says. "Look at me. Just look at me."

When we pass Vasquez's room on the way back, the curtains are drawn across the window. At the sight of the light green against the glass, I am so tired I want to collapse into my hospital bed or, better yet, my bed at home, the one I haven't even allowed myself to dream of since I came to. I want to pull my soft cotton sheets over my head and wake up again when I am more than an ache.

It is not to be.

Things really get cracking around here in the afternoons, and it's about one thirty now. Madame, my ballet teacher since I was five, owner of Cherryville Dance and former Manhattan

Ballet dancer of impeccable professional reputation, is in my room waiting for me with her usual chestnut bun, her tailored, stylish clothes in neutral colors, her light, flowery perfume. She's sitting next to Digby, who looks like he would love to melt into oblivion, he's so uncomfortable. I don't blame him. She adds stiffness to the place. Pressure. Not because she's a jerk or anything, but because seeing Madame in this crappy hospital room is like spotting a unicorn in a mall.

She's brought me a box wrapped in shiny silver paper, which she places on my lap when I don't take it from her. It's an early Christmas gift, she says.

When Sally comes in to take my blood pressure, she surveys the scene. Sally is nice to everyone who comes in, but not warm, though she hums friendly tunes in spite of herself. As far as I can tell, she likes it better when things are quiet and calm, one or two people around at most. I think it's because of her life at home, because all her kids and grandkids are always around.

As Madame begins to speak, of dance, of commitment, of what it takes to make it, Sally raises her eyebrows and snorts audibly, but I know Madame isn't trying to be harsh. The way her eyes skitter up and down across my body, the way her eyelids flutter, I see she's trying her best to adjust to this new, meeker version of me. And it's not just that. Things were strained between us before the accident. They were unclear.

34

I wish my jaunt to the other side had deleted my trip to New York with Madame from my memory, because sometimes you get time and perspective on something and realize you're a total moron.

Yes. That.

That day, I was dizzy with excitement that I had been invited to take class with the Bolshoi. The *Bolshoi*. This was my fate, my destiny, or the beginning of it anyway. I was sure of it. The Bolshoi hardly ever come to the U.S., but Madame's friend was running a special session in New York and they were in town for a couple of days, so she arranged the whole thing.

I spent days preening like a monumental asshat.

Of course the Bolshoi would notice my talent. Naturally they would tell me not even to bother packing a bag, that we would leave New York at once to go on a worldwide tour. They would buy me all new things, a wardrobe to complement my talent. My mother would cry, my father would disappear into the garage, my friends and I would weep together. No matter. The Bolshoi would provide me with a fainting couch upon which to grieve. Eventually everyone would understand the pressures of greatness and why I had to abandon them.

I'm almost blushing thinking about it, but it's a discomfort that lives coiled in between my ribs, not in my face. It's a good thing, or I'd have to self-immolate.

Madame and I went to New York together on the train. All the dots in the natural trajectory of my life assembled in a neat, efficient row. I had only to stay on the line. But what do you do when the line moves without warning?

Because when I got to the class, I had never seen the steps the dancers were doing, definitely hadn't ever performed them. They were exact, precise. I floundered, fumbled, too embarrassed to admit to my lack. Finally Madame's friend whispered to me, as I sweated and heaved disgracefully, that I was welcome to sit out until they practiced something at my level. I took one look at Madame and ran back to the subway station alone.

My legs were never so long. I was never so small. I ignored Madame's calls for days, and then . . . the river. If I had actually been the prodigy she claimed, that class could have led to all sorts of things. Maybe a summer with the Bolshoi, maybe more. It's the worst to see yourself, stupid and green, strutting around, thinking you're so everything, being sure of it even, only to find you're nothing and no one cares, that everything you thought about yourself was something you made, not based on reality. You're just a small-town girl with small-town nothing talent to match, dreaming lies about what life will be, like every sad, pathetic teenager in the world. And when you see it, really see it and accept it, the whole universe deflates.

The end.

So Madame sits at my bedside, chats with my mother, my brother, about nonsense. About the weather, *Peter Pan,* the new up-and-coming students who, between Madame and my mother and the lamppost, she says, do not and cannot and will never compare with me. She doesn't mention that terrible day with the Bolshoi in New York, and takes my fingers into hers so I know I'm forgiven, or at least pitied. I try to be here with her, but feel myself fade away, backwards through the sheets, the mattress, the floor, to the building's foundation, into the center of the earth. I'm grateful no one expects me to speak.

I don't know if I'll ever dance again. I don't know if I can, if I want to. In protest or agreement, I can't tell which, my legs electrocute me, twitch me back with pain. I tuck them in closer, hold on to my elbows.

Finally Madame leaves. The pain subsides.

Reggie bursts in not too long after, still sweaty from his workout, with some wilted flowers I'm sure he swiped out of his mom's trash, which he has squeezed into an empty Coke bottle. He cracks stupid jokes, then tells me I'm a total dud to hang out with since I can't talk like I used to, and then he lets out some fat tears, after which he and Digby leave to shoot hoops.

I'm unconscious within minutes.

The docs say my recovery depends a lot on nutrition, so

when I wake up, a green smoothie awaits. I get them every couple of hours. It takes a long time to drink. Lots of concentration. I have had awful, long, choking coughing fits that are so bad I would almost rather not eat. But I'm so hungry.

"Good job, baby," Rita says, when she comes for my empty glass. "I was worried about you. Sometimes the concussions lose their appetites, but you're going to be fine."

The Concussions. Like we're a band. Worst band ever.

"Thanks, Rita," I whisper.

This is the time of day when things get quiet in the hospital, when the nurses are the loudest ones. At seven, when the shift change happens and I lose Sally and gain Rita, they gossip.

This is when I listen closely enough to find out Rita is recently divorced and has a thing going with a male nurse named Alex, but how it's so damn hard to date when you work all night and he works the shifts you don't. It's also when I find out about Sally and her kids. She has six, and they all live with her, even though most of them are grown, so there's always something going on, especially with her son Jake. He's trouble.

But it's not only that. Now, after visitors and before the bedtime doings, is when I have Vasquez to myself, space to wonder about her life as I watch the ventilator breathe for her from the hallway. I could ask what happened to her, I know. All it would take is one question. I could find out her name, where she came from, all about her accident. But I don't want to, because here, like this, she's mine and we're almost the same.

Curtains back, the beige room is revealed. It hums and fusses like an organism. I think of a snake's insides constricting against its prey, muscular and deadly.

"Go ahead." Sally startles me.

I didn't know she was here, observing me with her umbrella in hand and an absurd teal kerchief on her head.

"Going home?" I whisper, and my throat chafes, but it's something.

"You bet. Time to start the day, part two."

It's raining outside. I can hear the pitter-patter tickling vaguely in the distance.

"You can go in there." She winks at me. "Talk to her. Tell her about your day. Whatever you want. Or not." She ticks my cheek, then opens the door for me. "I'll see you tomorrow, bright and early."

It's my first time in Vasquez's room. I feel like there's a conveyor belt leading me to her, not like I'm taking troubled steps. I glide to her bedside. The machines pump all around. I sit in Hudson's chair. Being this close to her frightens me, like I could be blinded or sucked into some kind of portal. I could get ejected into another dimension. It's like staring into the sun. Flowers are stacked on the tables at either side of her bed.

They're majestic and lean toward each other like they're deep in conversation.

"Hey," I say to Vasquez. "I'm Eden. Fellow coma girl. Pleased to meet you."

Bleep, bleep, bleep.

I clear my throat.

"You remember me? We met in the water." I glance around to be sure we're totally alone. "So, uh, where are you right now?" I say, stupidly. "Can you hear my voice?"

There's white crusted at the side of her mouth. I want to wipe it away, but I have nothing wet enough, so I leave it there and try not to stare at it.

"I never cared about life after death," I say carefully, forcing my voice to weave around the words. "When you're dead you're dead. It's what makes sense. Mom and Dad said don't believe in fairy tales. But what is that place, Vasquez, with the flowers? It's real, right? Because you're here and you were there, so it has to be. Are you still wherever?" My lip trembles. I wait for it to stop, breathing heavy from the effort of so much speaking. "Are you in the In Between?"

Vasquez doesn't answer me.

"I'm jealous," I say, finally. "Jealous of you."

A WEEK AFTER THAT, ON DECEMBER 19, IT'S OUR BIRTHDAY.

Today, Digby and I are eighteen and having a party in my hospital room. It's only four o'clock, so it's not like anyone is getting their socks knocked off or anything. Everyone came straight from school or home, shucked coats into a pile on the floor, unwrapped wax paper treats. Sally poured some coffee for my parents and made me a shake. Vanilla-flavored, like this shindig.

Parker, Reggie, Digby, Lucille, Wrenny, my parents, and me. Everyone who matters shoved into a three-hundred-square-foot room. Mom brought in one of those Bluetooth speakers and Digby made a playlist, but when the music came on, it vibrated through me with unfriendly electricity, and my body went rigid. The music was too hard, too tight.

So now there's nothing to listen to but the murmur of voices.

Digby and Lucille, boiled, cooked, so deep into each other, sit in a single chair in the corner, she perched on his lap like

41

a miniature poodle, hair in a ponytail, perpetually flushed, clothes draped from her shoulder like they want to come off, as his fingers search for her ear, her waist, resting only for a moment at her stomach, then off again, looking for the next thing.

They make me seasick and embarrassed for my parents, who are studying the particulars of the hospital room décor with special intensity, Wren huddled into them like the proxy family they are.

It's hard not to gawk at Digby and Lucille, shining like they do, but it's not polite to stare, so I end up feeling manipulated, because this room is small and where do they want me to put my eyes?

"Somebody get a hose," Reggie says, plopping down next to me. "For shame, people."

Parker settles himself behind Reggie and munches on a huge piece of cake, staring into space. Park has always had this shaggy blond hair, shiny, soft girl hair, and he has gathered it into a bun which now sits at the top of his head. He's also growing some kind of sad scruff on his chin. He is always in his basketball jersey. Funny the things you get to know about people. Like how Parker likes little dogs and went vegetarian when he saw a documentary about the food industry. How he couldn't stop bawling for days. And what will happen when Reggie stops talking for the both of them? Will Park have anything to say?

42

"I cannot with that anymore," Reggie says, ticking his head toward the writhing chair. "We should lock them in a room till they start to annoy each other so we can all go back to normal. I'm all for love, but they're getting porno."

I swish the straw around in the now-separating milkshake.

"You want me to throw some of your cake in a blender?" he asks. "Bad luck not to eat the cake."

"That's weddings, not birthdays," I say. "I'm good."

This year's birthday cake is a triple-layer yellow with vanilla frosting, both our names perfectly written in icing across the top. Mom always makes our cakes, of course.

Last year was a ballet slipper cake for me, a basketball one for Digby, like we were still seven and just beginning to be defined by the things we like to do. This cake smells like butter and lemon. It smells like home.

"Fine," Reggie says. "Don't drink your damn cake. You don't have to be all grumpy."

"I'm not grumpy."

"Is it because you're an old lady now?"

I'm older than Reggie by three months.

"Idiot," I croak.

"I'm just glad you're done tripping," he says. "You were like one of those people who drop bad drugs and think they can fly." He takes a huge bite. "It was funny, though." He clutches

43

at his chest. "No! No! They're coming for me! The flowers are going to take me back!"

Flashes.

Me screaming.

Me trying to tell my parents about the flowers, about Vasquez, about the black petals underwater.

"I need some air," I say.

I KNEW HE WOULD
BE HERE, AND THAT'S
SUPER WEIRD.

*Hudson is in the quiet of the hall-*way, outside Vasquez's window where I usually am. Maybe I came back from the In Between with psychic powers, a sixth sense. That would be almost as great as being a hauntish ghost. I will the painting across from me to fly off the wall. Nothing happens.

Disappointing.

Actually, now that I think about it, Hudson's here most days at the same time. This time. So . . . yeah. Not so psychic.

"What are you doing?" he calls.

I twitch so hard he laughs. He's far enough away from me that his laughter sounds hollow and distant.

"Easy." His hands are out in front of him. "I didn't mean to scare you."

I shuffle in his direction, my family's and friends' voices fading to a dull buzz behind me as I get farther from the room. The closer I get to him, the more I wonder why I'm moving

45

toward him instead of scurrying away. I mean, I don't know him. We stand side by side and look in the room. No change in Vasquez. She's still sleeping, Snow White's poison apple still lodged in her throat.

"We did homework together." He nods toward her. "Every day."

"Oh," I say.

"Yeah, we both work a lot, but she would come over every night when her shift was done, or I would go to her place. And then, we would—I don't know—listen to music or whatever, and quiz each other and stuff."

"Yeah," I say.

"It's her birthday," he says.

I'm stunned. Like, super stunned.

This piece of information makes me feel completely different about my own birthday, like I'm so lucky to even have one, like I should be in my room with a smile on, hanging out with my family, being grateful and whatnot.

"Eighteen," he says. "She was waiting for this day for a long time." He smiles. "Always mad that my birthday is in September. Every year: bitter." This makes him smile again, and I can see her, Vasquez, telling him happy birthday and punching him in the arm in the same breath.

"I don't know what to do without her," he says. "You know how if you chew gum when you study, you're supposed to chew it when you're testing? It's like that, I guess, having her gone, except about a lot of stuff. I don't know what's what without her. We've been together since we were little kids."

I get it. I'm the same with my friends.

His face contorts. I want to say, *How many friends do you have?* I want to ask if he's really as lost and lonely as he seems.

"Why are you out here?" I say. "Instead of in there with her."

"I don't know," he says. "Today I can't make myself open the door." His lip trembles, and his eyes fill. He puts a hand on the window. "Some days are like that. Some days I can't even make myself come at all."

I want to touch his back, to comfort him, but before I can do anything that stupid, Lucille appears in the hall with a piece of cake on a lavender paper plate. She starts toward me, then catches sight of Hudson and backs up, out of sight.

"Sorry," I say.

"Is that your room?"

I sigh. It's loud, involuntary, and I feel much better after.

"My family is here," I say. "That's my best friend . . . my brother's girlfriend. Whichever."

47

"Is that odd?" he says.

"You know," I say, "thank you for saying that. It *is* odd. Especially since we're twins. Don't you think him boning my bestie presents a conflict of interest?"

He shrugs. "Maybe. Guess it mostly depends how you take it."

"Yeah," I say. "Anyway, they're here because it's my birthday. Our birthday, I mean. Mine and my brother's. Too."

It takes saying it out loud to realize how totally weird it is that Vasquez has the same birthday. *This* is odd. Odder.

"It's your birthday?" He runs his hand through his hair and squinches his forehead. "Seriously? Today?"

"Yeah," I say. "Eighteen. Yay, me!"

Nice, Eden. Very nice, you insensitive imbecile.

"Yay you," he says, trying for a smile. "Happy birthday." He looks back through the window while I grapple with a fine mix of guilt, embarrassment, and sadness. "That is crazy though. Same birthday."

"Don't it just beat all?" I need duct tape for my mouth. I should re-lose my voice.

"It does," Hudson says, glancing at me sidelong, like he wouldn't believe me if it weren't for Lucille and her lavender plate.

"You want some cake?" I say. This conversation is getting

48

too crazy for me. "My mom made it. She's good at that. You can have my piece. I can't . . ."

"Naw," he says. When he waves me away, I smell green on him, like chlorophyll, something clean. "Thanks, but if she can't have any on her own birthday, I'm not going to either."

"As a recently comatose person, I can tell you you're thinking all wrong," I say. "You don't have to eat my birthday cake, but think for a minute. If you were her and she was you, wouldn't you want her to do something to celebrate?"

He stares blankly.

"Okay, that was convoluted."

"Kind of."

"Well still, what's her favorite?"

"Favorite what?"

"Cake."

"Chocolate," he says without hesitation. "Chocolate sour cream cake from the Italian restaurant where she works. They put it on the menu for her. I don't think it's very Italian. She basically bullied them into doing it so she could have it whenever she wanted."

"So get some of that. I'm sure she would like you to do that. If I were her," I say, "I would want you to. For me. If I couldn't."

He leans against the wall and watches me for so long I kind

of want to flip him off. Anything to break the tension and his stare.

"Yeah," he says, after so much time has passed I've forgotten what we were even talking about. "Maybe so."

From Almost Dead: True Stories of the Afterlife

I died when I fell off the roof of my childhood home in Maine. I was eight. It was a stupid thing to do, climbing on the roof like that, but my big brother Tommy and I wanted to watch the meteor shower. He was nimble. I never was. The house was three stories with the attic.

I broke my neck. My senses faded one by one, that's what I remember best. That sort of gentle whiteout. Hearing, then smell, then I couldn't feel anything at all. Sight was last to go.

I was ejected out of my body and floating for a matter of seconds. I came to, then went back to white a few more times. I was reinserted into my body, like a real uncomfortable pop. All the pain came back. I remember that, too. Months in a full-body cast. Learning to walk all over again, like a baby taking first steps.

Lucky I wasn't a quadriplegic. But I guess it was good for something. I always try to tell people who've lost loved ones. There's no pain after. The pain only comes before. Whatever else there is, you can believe that.

— *Marty Conescu, 72, retired builder*

I'M THREE DAYS POST-BIRTHDAY, AND I'M OUT OF HERE.

The doctor takes notes. This is the same neurologist I've been seeing since I woke up, the one who's shorter than me and has Sasquatch-hairy arms and no ring on his wedding finger, which doesn't necessarily mean anything for most people, but for him I think it does. I bet he has no furniture in his house—or no—apartment, and a car with doors that close with bungee cords because they're broken and he never has time to get them fixed because he's at the hospital too much to go to the body shop and have work done. I bet he once had friends, not many, but some, and now he doesn't, but that's okay because he's really good at his job and does brain surgery and saves people all the time, and that's how he keeps from being dead inside.

Once you start making up stories about people, it's hard to stop.

The doc hands me a third drink, the one Sally just mixed

up. I try not to be angry at her for that. This is the thickest, nastiest one yet. Swallow therapy. Swallow torture.

"You can sit on the bed," he says. "You'll be more comfortable."

"No thanks," I say.

He nods dismissively, obviously uninterested in the particulars. That, or he's used to me doing the opposite of what he says by now.

Contrarian, Dad calls me.

I've made progress. I don't feel like I'm going to die from drinking, my voice is working better, and earth doesn't feel like an evil, angry strobe light anymore.

I size up the paper cup in front of me, stare at the bubbly, goopy pink. Fake cherry is my least favorite. Except maybe for banana, or (ugh) pineapple, which I have told the nurses is unacceptable.

"Take all the time you need," the doc says. He flips his wrist and glances at his watch, which is silver with a black strap and Roman numerals.

"Okay, let's do this," I say, trying not to think about oozing sludge as it slides down my throat. I give a few pre-swallows and get a couple of sips down without a choking episode.

"Look at that smile." Sally claps her hands.

"Life is about small victories." That's what they tell me, anyway.

"My little miracle patient." Sally appears satisfied, like she was the one who drank kill slime.

"Excellent." The doc writes down facts in black ink with a nice fountain pen. "I'm going to get the discharge papers together, and then you should be ready to join your family."

He looks up at me, waiting.

"Should we discuss your aftercare instructions now?"

I keep forgetting I'm eighteen now, and I can do all sorts of things on my own that I couldn't do before.

"Go ahead," I say, as Sally brings me a glass of water.

"Small sips with that," he says. "Remember it's easier to aspirate thin liquids than thick ones."

I nod. They reexplain this to me every time I drink.

"Okay, then," he says. "A couple of things, Miss Jones. You'll need to make sure you take in enough calories, which is a challenge on a liquid diet. So, six of the shakes we prescribed per day, at two-hour intervals, regardless of solid food intake. You can get creative. Make smoothies and juices as needed. Then move on to mashed potatoes, pureed carrots, that sort of thing. You'll work your way up. It will take some time, but you will get through it. Frustration is a part of this process, but it won't last forever."

"Old people diet," I say. "Got it."

"That's right," he says. "It is an absolute priority that you get your weight back to normal. It will take some time, but —"

"Consistency is the key to results," I say.

"Right again. You'll have physical therapy in the adjacent building five days a week for six weeks and then we will reevaluate. Let's see if we can get you dancing again, eh?" He makes brief eye contact. "I hear you were something."

Something.

"And as you know, when you have a head injury such as yours, there can be some depression, some anxiety, dizziness, lack of appetite, dissociation —"

"Hooray," I say.

"Yes, well." He hands me a card. *Marlene Gat,* it says, and then some numbers, an email address. "I'm recommending you see a therapist once a week. Trauma such as yours requires emotional support. We have a lovely staff. I've spoken with your parents about it, and they're in agreement it's a good idea. I think Dr. Gat would be an excellent fit for you. So you'll be back here for that as well."

"Why leave?" I say. "Maybe I can put a cot in a closet. Move in with you guys. You can slip me a tray every now and then."

He looks up from his notes.

"That would not be advisable," he says. "You need to begin to reintegrate into your own life. You've made sufficient progress for release, and of course you'll want to be at home to enjoy the holidays with your family." He takes off his glasses, wipes them, puts them back on. "You are indeed a bit of a miracle, Eden, bouncing back as you are, and we don't want miracles languishing in here unnecessarily. The main thing is to be gentle with yourself. Healing is going to take time, much more than you would like. Take life at a slow pace. Smell the flowers, as they say . . . I'm recommending some time at home before you attempt school. I hear your teachers are willing to work with you to see that you graduate on schedule. And one last thing: no unnecessary activity without permission from your physical therapist."

No dancing.

"Sally," he says, "would you get me Mrs. Wesley's chart? We'll go see her next."

"Sure," she says. "Be right back."

"I've noticed, Miss Jones," the doc says when Sally's gone, "that you have been spending some time down the hall." He glances toward Vasquez's room. "That's excellent," he says. "Very helpful." He looks out to the nurses' station then back to me. "We don't know why yet, but the presence of other people seems to be important in recovery when it comes to comas. Human touch. It's a nice thing to do for someone like her." He peers over his glasses as I wonder what "someone like her" means exactly. "You know," he says, "many years ago, I was in a coma for seven days. I had people by my bedside who held on to me until I woke up. My mother, my father, my sister. That may have helped me to come back."

This is an unexpected turn of events. Coma patient turned coma doc. And the servant becomes the master.

"You say you came back," I say. "From where, exactly?"

Was he In Between? What did his look like? Maybe it's tailor-made to each person's memories and specifications. I wonder, did he bring something back with him too?

"We'll save that story for another day." He extends his hand as Sally comes back in holding a stack of clipboards, which she gives to him. "Well, good luck, Miss Jones. And don't hesitate to be in touch should the need arise."

Everything in me tightens and threatens. I don't want to let him go.

Sally pats me on the back when he's gone.

"We call him Spock," she says. "Not a lick of humor, but he's a sharp one. Not as cold as he seems."

I hug her hard, so hard she throws up her arms like I'm attacking her and she needs to protect herself. But when the surprise wears off, she gives in and rests her arms on my back.

"Good God," she says, finally, tapping me away from her. "I don't know what anyone's worried about. You got your strength all right. You're ready to go."

I follow her from the room and lean my elbow on the tall part of the nurse desk as she gets a juice and some ice chips and concocts a hospital slushie. She sits down heavily on her yoga ball chair, which looks really strange but which she claims loudly and regularly is a godsend.

"What's going on with Jake?" I ask, as I take a sip of apple-y goodness.

Jake is Sally's son, the one who's trouble. He has a girlfriend Sally doesn't like. Her name is Rhonda. Sally says they smoke pot, and Rhonda wears half shirts and short shorts at the same time, which everyone knows you can do one or the other, but never both. They get up to no good in Jake's room while all the kids and grandkids are home trying to act normal. Sally's daughter Tina lets her know what's going on.

Sally bounces on her yellow yoga ball. "Now, see, I spend all my time working so I don't have to think about those damn kids and the fact that they're adults and I can't get rid of a one of them, and you come over here asking me about Jake." Her words don't match her tone, which is weirdly affectionate. "He's a hot mess, that's what. Total failure to launch. I told Tina he's not to go in that room with that girl and close the door. He wants to get frisky out of wedlock, he needs to get his own house, pay his own rent."

"Right," I say. "Totally."

She grabs a file and opens it, rifles some papers around and then slaps it shut. I have agitated her. "So what do you think? You ready for real life, duck?"

Mom, Dad, Digby, Lucille. They'll all be here soon to take me home. My things are in the duffel bag at my feet, including the pink blanket from my bed that I once hated, but have since grown attached to, and am now stealing. My room looks like any other hospital room. No more mess. No more signs of life. I've only been out for two minutes, and someone is already in there, disinfecting things.

"Is that what this is?" I say. I pick at the fake gifts on the fake miniature Christmas tree on the desk. "Real life?"

"As close as any of us can make out," she says. "I'll tell you one thing, though. Working in this part of the hospital, you have to be prepared for people to pass away all the time. Mostly the elderly, thank heavens." She looks skyward. "But you don't get attached when you're me. You learn about life and death, learn it good. And when you have a girl like you in here, stunning and with everything ahead of her, and you don't know if she's going to make it and then she does, you want her to do the best possible job, because lord knows, not everyone gets that chance."

"With great power comes great responsibility," I say.

"Something like that."

"No pressure," I say.

"Well," Sally says. "What do I know? Oh!" She reaches under her desk. "We got you something. I almost forgot."

She hands me a package wrapped in red holiday paper with candy canes on it. It's squishy.

"It's from all of us, but especially from me and Rita."

I hold the gift tight under my arm. I don't open it because if I do, I will unzip from sternum to tailbone and all my bits will spill out. It will be messy.

"I didn't mean to scare you, hon. About the real world. You're going to do great," Sally says. "Out there."

Today her scrubs have turtles on them.

"I know the hospital is going to be boring without me," I say, finally, "but you're just going to have to try to get by."

She raises an eyebrow.

"It's okay, Sally. You can admit I've been the light of your life. I mean, aside from Jake."

"Well," she says, smooshing her finger between the prongs of a paper clip, "maybe that's so. Although, you've got an unfair advantage over most of the other patients in here, what with the consciousness and all. You being my favorite has nothing to do with personality."

"I knew I was your favorite!" I say, as Mrs. Wesley, the stroke lady whose room was two down from mine, wheels by, head locked at what looks like a painful angle. I look at the clock over Sally's head. "How long do I have till they come?"

"Should be here any second," Sally says. "Your dad said they were on their way."

It's twenty minutes from Cherryville to here. I picture them all in Mom's van, singing road songs, playing road games. I see my fluffy dog, Beaver Cleaver, BC for short, sitting in his crate at home, tail slapping against the floor. He always knows when something exciting is afoot. He'll be waiting for me.

I don't know why leaving the hospital feels like such a big deal. I've only been awake a couple of weeks, although technically I've been here for six if you include the coma. The thing is, aside from the hugeness of the world leaving me panicked at my own comparative smallness, I don't want to abandon Vasquez. What's she going to do here without me?

Same thing she's doing now, Eden. She's going to do nothing.

"I'll be back." I slurp the last of my juice and nod down the hall. "Make sure none of the other coma patients steals my bag."

"I'll get right on that," Sally says.

Not being able to walk well makes you aware of all the bones and joints, and the neurons that have to fire in order to take a single step. Sally must be watching me teeter away, stiff as the Tin Man. I see myself lifting off in a grand jeté, and it's like that happened to someone else. Had to have, because now, each lift of the leg, each hinge of the hip, is felt. Not arduous like it was when I first woke up, but noticed, noticeable. I used to be able to fly, and I didn't even know it. I'd like to go back in time and slap myself a lot.

I stop in front of Vasquez's window, room 210. I stare at her, as is my custom.

"Hey again."

Hudson, who I didn't notice come in, is in my face.

"Do you know her or something?" he asks. "I mean, why do you stand here? I thought I knew everyone she did. Does. Did."

"I met her when I was under," I say. "We shook hands in purgatory."

He scrunches his eyebrows.

"Kidding," I say. "But I feel like I know her. Coma bonding?"

He nods like this is an acceptable answer and turns back.

Do I know her? I want to say. *I mean, of course I know her. She is Vasquez. Badass, confident, stylish in her own way, obsessed with finding*

new underground bands, secret musician herself, dreams of being a pro-
moter. Someone stabbed her in a jealous rage, and she fell and hit her head
on the side of the stage by the mosh pit, which is how she wound up here.
Right?

Instead of letting my mouth loose, I stay quiet and assess him while he is staring hypnotically forward.

Hudson's in an army green jacket, a black and white flannel on underneath, cradling white roses wrapped in newspaper like they're an infant. The cold is still latched to him, and it reminds me that there is an outside. He smells fresh, but not detergent fresh. That green again. Actual nature, trees, soil, leaves fresh.

I swallow.

"Your staring is kind of aggressive," he says, and as he does, a luscious black petal falls from the ceiling and floats to the floor between us.

"So is your tone," I say, as it disappears into the floor.

Something about redheads: there's no camouflaging a blush.

"Sorry," he says. "I didn't mean to have a tone. It's just everything is weird right now, including you, no offense." He shuffles. "So, are you in high school?" he asks.

Aw, he's trying to make small talk.

"Senior," I say. "I was anyway. Not sure what I am now. Maybe a high school dropout."

"Me too. Not a dropout. A senior." He is tripping over his words and reddening too. I'm so glad I don't have to be awkward alone.

"I'm getting out today," I offer. "Of here, I mean."

"You say that like it's prison."

"Food's better."

"You like the hospital food?" he says.

"I like smelling it."

"For real?"

"Don't be a hater," I say. "I can't eat yet. I'm starving." I nonlaugh. Because it's nonfunny.

"Have you been to prison?" he says after a second.

"What?"

"You said that the food's better than in prison. Have you been to prison?"

"My life isn't that interesting," I say. "You?"

"Not personally. And don't sell yourself short. You're a twin, and you were in a coma," he says, ticking each item on his fingers. "That's interesting."

"I guess. But now I'm awake."

As far as I know.

"And now you're out of here."

"Yup, just like that. Poof! It's like I was never here at all."

"You should bundle up," he says. "It's so cold out there. A

bitter day. Windy and cold, not just cold." He shakes his head slightly, as though having some sort of internal discussion between himself and himself. "Sorry," he says. "I'm not awesome at talking."

"Oh," I say, thinking that's adorable. That he said it, and that it's so. Double-dorable.

He moves to open the door.

"Why are all the flowers white?" I say. "The ones you bring."

"Because that's what we grow," he says. "My parents own the flower shop in town."

I nod.

"Flower Power, it's called." He shifts the bundle from one arm to the other. It really does look like a baby. "My stepmom, she only likes white flowers. She has a stand downstairs. My dad mans the store. I work wherever they need me."

"I know," I say, and he looks at me sharply.

I've seen him. On my wanderings in the hospital lobby, which are frowned upon, but which I've been indulging in anyway.

"I mean, I'm not stalking you or anything. I've seen you at the stand."

"I've seen you too," he says. "Next time you should come say hi."

"Maybe I will."

"Instead of acting like you don't know me at all."

I smile. "You didn't say anything to me either."

"I don't like being rejected," he says, in a way that makes me certain he has never experienced rejection even once. "Anyway, you never came close enough. There's only so many times I'm going to yell for you across a room."

My face is legitimately about to burst into flames.

He turns the knob on Vasquez's door like he's going to go in, but then hesitates. "What's your name?" he says. "You never told me."

"It's Eden," I say, and shoot my hand out to meet his.

He takes it, but we don't really shake.

"Hey, Eden," he says.

"What's your name?"

I ask it, but I almost don't want to know. The second he tells me and it's not Hudson, everything I've made up about him and Vasquez will go away, and then I'll be left with nothing but truth.

"It's Joe," he says, and I buoy instead of deflate, because he is such a Joe, and because that is the perfect name for him.

And her?

"That's Jasmine."

"Jasmine?"

"Legally. No one calls her that," he says. "Everyone calls her Jaz."

That's better. More right.

So what happened to her? And why does she have that scar? Are you related? Is she your girl? Why don't her parents come? How long has she been here? How is her brain?

Quiet, self.

I could ask Rita or Sally, I guess. I could probably ask anyone on this floor, and they would tell me something about her. About Jasmine. Jaz.

"We're awkwardly holding hands," I say.

"What's awkward about it?" he says, but he flushes and drops it.

He doesn't move, though, even when the double doors whip open and my family is upon us. Instead he looks like maybe he has questions filtering through his mind, too.

"Got your bag?" Dad looks freshly bathed and bright, and is swathed in cashmere and some sort of soapy scent.

"Nurses' station." I point. "Sally has it."

"Ready to go, honey?" Mom says. "Ready for home?"

When I think of it, it's my old house that runs through my head, my quilt, my old posters, my creaky floorboards, where I could tap on the wall and Lucille or Wren would answer every time. But then I remember I'll be going home to the new place. The clean and marbled one that smells like my parents' successes.

"Sure."

Joe is paying close attention to everything, and he flinches slightly when my mom puts her arms around me and squeezes.

Lucille hugs me, too, gingerly. "So excited," she says. "You're coming home! Yay!" She pauses to look at Joe. "Hey," she says. "Lucille."

I don't know why, but I don't want her to look at him, to talk to him.

"Joe," he says.

"Have you seen the doctor?" Mom says, like he's not standing there. She seems like maybe she's having a manic episode.

"Chill," I say. "Everything is taken care of. He's getting papers."

"And did he talk to you about therapy?" Mom and Lucille exchange looks.

Joe ducks into Jaz's room, giving me a wave. That's right. Run from Crazytown as fast as you can.

"That's my private business," I say to Mom, as soon as the door is completely closed. "And I don't feel like talking about it."

"My, my, aren't we sassy today?" Mom says. "I'll call the doctor later, then."

I sigh a lot, and loudly in her direction.

Digby is next to me, and then Dad with my bag. "News bulletin, Fam: I don't feel like talking about my mental health with any of you, okay? I'm tired. I want to go home and see my dog. And I'm fine."

I don't tell them how the window to Jasmine's room is suddenly alive and writhing with flowers so thick I can't even see inside.

"Okaaay then, sensitive," Digby says. "You ready to go?"

My dad offers his arm, so I thread my hand through and lean.

"Yeah," I say. "I'm ready."

But I'm not.

DURING

(january)

I SHOULD MARK MY BEDROOM WALL LIKE THEY DO IN PRISON MOVIES.

Tick. Monday. Tick. Tuesday. Tick. Tick. Tick. Two and a half weeks out of the hospital, almost five weeks since I woke up.

It's Wren's night to cook, so Digby and I are on our way over to Lucille's. On Wren's cooking night, she gets to choose pretty much anything she wants, as long as Lucille can afford it. Digby helps out, and Mom sends over a bag of food sometimes. Even Lucille's boss, Fred, contributes.

They do it because Wren's school counselor says it's good for her to feel a sense of accomplishment and to create a sanctuary, a sense of security, since their parents' leaving was a "sanctuary violation," as in once they felt safe and cared for in their home no matter how unstable it actually was, and now they actually know that safety and security are an illusion, so it's important to rebuild that illusion so everyone concerned can be normal, even though they know a deep dark human truth now and can't ever really unknow it: that things change in a minute, without warning, and you have to cope. At least, Digby says, they have help, community and all that. They're going to be okay now, no matter what happens. They have so many people behind them, around them.

Digby's doing a lot of talking, which is a good thing, because I'm still not totally used to being outside yet. The hospital was a self-contained concrete block that held all my necessities. Now my house has become the same. Outside, there's a storm brewing, with angry clouds, the wind so vicious I can feel it shaking Beast as we rumble down the hill and the whole world trembles.

So once a week, Digby goes on telling me, oblivious to my tremors, they all cook and eat together over there instead of separately, or up at our place. I press my cheek against the truck and think how I know that truth Digby's talking about, too. One day I was standing in the most familiar place, and then a second later, I was almost dead, and nothing has felt right since. Same for Wren and Lucille. One day they were regular kids with two parents and everything, and then in a heartbeat, in the time it took their dad to lock his hands around their mom's throat and almost choke her, it was over, and nothing was ever the same. They didn't author the thing that changed their lives. They didn't choose it. We have that in common. We all have some version of it to deal with.

74

I only move when Digby opens the door on my side and I almost fall out.

"You okay?" he says.

"Oh, yeah," I say, "peachy."

I don't look at my old door, at the rocking chair where my old porch swing used to hang, at the railing between the two houses where Lucille and I left messages and books for each other when we were little.

The house I used to live in is falling into the ground like it's sitting in quicksand—at least that's how it feels. It's run-down and dusty, no matter how clean, because it's about 150 years old (there's a plaque on the outside that reads 1874, so I'm only exaggerating a tiny bit). That used to drive my parents crazy, that no matter how much they redid our half of the house, it always felt like it was one solid shake away from crumbling into oblivion. It's why they moved, why they built the new house. Still, as soon as I'm through the door of Lucille's, something comes over me that's as familiar as my own name, so sweet my teeth ache.

Except she's moved stuff around.

The couch now sits against the wall in the living room instead of in the middle. The TV is gone, one of Lucille's paintings hangs in its place, some blue and orange swirly thing that makes no sense whatsoever, and the coffee table that has always been cluttered with magazines and remotes is clear except for a small silver vase that holds a single red rose. A guitar sits on a stand in the corner next to a beanbag, and a fresh rug with soft pile covers the floor, while a speaker plays Digby-style indie music. Incense burns, and a stew bubbles on the stove. The house doesn't even smell like it used to, like — I don't know — weed from the pot Lucille's parents thought they smoked so stealthily, and maple syrup from the pancakes Laura made when she was high on the aforementioned weed.

I'm stunned. Digby and Lucille have completely taken over. Moved in. Exorcised her parents so completely that, aside from the guitar, I see no trace of them anywhere.

Wren appears to be used to it, untraumatized. She assembles salads. A cucumber here, a tomato there, each carefully placed. Digby makes a fruit salad. My jock brother is balling melons.

Every time I turn around, I run into things.

Even though this is downright odd, I have to embrace it. My social options are currently limited, have been limited since I got out of the hospital. I can't play another game of gin with my dad or drink another cup of tea with my mom, or observe my parents for signs of permanent damage for one more minute. I can't lie in bed and stare at dance posters either, and old ballet shoes, or watch any more videos online about how to apply eyeliner or make the perfect coconut-based cleanser. Plus, I was barely conscious for Christmas. Hardly aware, too, when the ball came down announcing the New Year and a sea of black flowers rose up from the floor until I floated on them, into my room, through the night, and the next day and night again.

Time is speeding, speeding while I stand perfectly still. Also, I haven't gone anywhere besides the hospital since I left it, for physical therapy, to sit at Jasmine Vasquez's bedside as she withers. I realize that's stupid, which is why I'm here, and also why I'm going to attempt to go back to school tomorrow. I'm conscious and "thriving." That plus my begging got my parents to agree.

Wren wrestles an avocado seed out of its meat. Digby sets the coffee table, walking back and forth between the kitchen and the living room as needed. Lucille stirs her stew in a rhythm.

"You guys are like a clock," I say. "One of those ones with the wooden people that move back and forth while music plays when the hour changes."

"What?" Digby says. They all freeze and look up.

To my point.

"Nothing," I say. "Never mind." I tiny-sip on cool water in the corner as they discuss their lives.

"Tomorrow, you have to stay after school to set up your science fair project," Lucille turns her focus to Wren.

"I know." Wren fashions avocado slices into flower shapes and lays them on top of lettuce. "You don't have to tell me."

"I have to work at Fred's, so Digby's going to pick you up."

"Yeah, practice is done right at seven. I'll come find you at the gym," he says. "Where I will be congratulating you on your ribbon."

"Yeah, right." Wren pauses, looking up from her project. She suddenly looks small, as young as she actually is, instead of bold and big and confident. "Are you guys going to be mad at me if I don't win?"

"No!" Lucille says. "Oh my gosh, no."

"Of course we won't be mad," Digby says. "I don't know why they have the science fair the day you get back from vacation. That seems stupid."

"So we could work on it over the holidays," Wren says. "But we were so busy."

"Your project is great!" He swings his arms toward the charts. "Investigating the effects of the weather on mood? Awesomesauce. I'm just sorry we can't be there for the actual thing. And Mrs. A. has a check-up. Bad timing." He goes back to his busy work. "But I don't want you to go outside after dark." Digby gets stern. "I'll be there to pick you up, I promise."

"Okay," she says. "But you don't have to be paranoid. I'm ten. I could walk home."

"Wren!" Lucille says.

"I'm not saying I'm going to," she says. "I'm saying I could and it would be fine."

"It *might* be fine," Lucille corrects her.

"Nothing is ever certain," I say.

It gets a loud kind of quiet.

"Are you okay, Eden?" Digby says, with an edge of irritation.

"Existentially speaking, I mean," I go on. "When you really break it down, nothing is certain. Everything could fall apart at any time."

Lucille bites her lip and resumes stirring.

"Way to bring the heavy, Edes," Digby says. He slaps the plates down on the coffee table in the living room, stacks the bowls on top. The dining room table is covered in poster board and markers, and cardboard models, so we can't sit there.

"Parker's parents are out of town this weekend," Digby says, after an eternal minute.

"Again?" Lucille says.

"They're fools in love," Digby says, and he kisses Lucille on the top of her head. "Or, re-in-love. Park thinks his dad is making up for something. Either way, they've been out of town a lot." Digby pops a cherry tomato into his mouth. "Lucky for us. Party every weekend until they start fighting again."

"Yay." I hear how flat my voice is. "Beer pong and keg stands for everyone."

"Whatever," Digby says. "We only have a few months, then it's all done. After that, we'll be grownups and we will never see Parker puke in his yard again. We'll be busy being us."

Lucille pauses to stare at Digby, cranes her neck back, and smiles dizzily. It's because he said "we." He said "us." Lucille is no longer alone. I can't help it. I roll my eyes.

After an eon of besotted swooning, Lucille carries the stew to the table and pulls bread from the oven. We gather. I hope they can't hear my bones crack as I fold myself into a shape that fits.

"So, Friday?" Digby says.

"Yes," Lucille says. "I'm off from Fred's," she explains to me. "Freebird Fridays from now on. That means I have to work Wednesdays, but . . ."

"Since I have practice during the week," Digby continues her thought, "it's worth it. For us to have a weekend night off together," he finishes.

"Yeah," I say. "Of course."

I was only out a month right? Because they've been married

for centuries. I stare at the stew in front of me. Ninety percent chance of embarrassing choking episode. I have a shake in my bag. If I get it, am I being rude? Or actually, if I take small bites of carrot, work around the beef, I'll be fine. Brings my chances of choking down significantly.

"And me?" Wren says. "What do I do while you're at Parker's?"

"I can watch her," I say. I'm not ready for a party yet. A hundred people from school? School itself is going to be bad enough. "I'd rather hang with Wren."

"No!" Lucille says.

I try not to be offended, but it's offensive. I've been watching Wren forever and now Lucille doesn't trust me.

Digby's mouth, which has hinged open, the better to inhale his food with, cranks shut just as dramatically.

"Don't take it the wrong way, Eden. Mrs. A. has Wren," Lucille says. "That's all. We've got babysitting covered. Is what I mean."

"I'm so not a baby," Wren says, buttering some bread. "I don't need any of you."

"You should come to the party with us anyway." Digby resumes eating his bread. "Don't you want to see everybody?"

I pause. How do I say "no way not at all" nicely?

"Everybody wants to see you," Digby says. "They miss you. We miss you."

I mash a piece of potato into a smaller, flatter piece and test it in my mouth, scoot it to the back, and swallow carefully.

"Shoot," Lucille says. "I forgot, I got the blender out for you." She takes my bowl away and I hear a whirring noise. She returns my stew, a gravy-like brown. "I pureed it," she says, proudly.

"Thanks," I say.

"Oh." Wren peers at this upsetting version of my dinner and purses her lips. "I'm sorry, Eden. This is so not how my cooking night is supposed to go."

I take a bite while everyone watches, immobilized by discomfort. One more is all I can do. I'm not sure whether it's textural or psychological.

"It's my fault," Lucille says, glumly. "I'm the one who suggested stew. I thought it would be easier for you."

"It is," I say. "Easier than a lot of things."

I look at all of their crestfallen, droopy faces.

"What?" I say. "I have my trusty shake in my bag if I need it. No one's going to starve."

"Those shakes are so gross." Digby shudders. "They taste like plastic and depression, like someone who's never eaten chocolate decided to make chocolate."

"Dig, stop," Lucille says. Then to me: "Do you want me to make you a smoothie or something? It does kind of look like dog food."

"I'm good," I say. "Really."

"How long until you can eat normal?" Wren says.

"I've been doing some practicing." I tinker with my fork. "It's getting better. Little by little." I echo Dr. Patel, my physical therapy man.

"Okay," Lucille says, but she sags. "Theory proven. I do suck. I'm sorry."

"Hey," I say, "it's okay. I don't mind. It's like being a baby again." I remember those thick, pasty, tester shakes Spock made me drink in the hospital. Anything is better than that.

But something trembles in me, travels in a direct line from below my belly button into my throat. Something that says I don't belong here, that this is no longer my place. Seems like Digby and Lucille and Wren feel it too, because we eat the rest of the meal in silence.

REGGIE WAITS IN
MY DRIVEWAY.

He's in a down jacket and jeans,
tall and bulky, hair big and curly. I spy Parker in Reggie's car's
tiny back seat, doing something on his phone. He doesn't get
out.

"I have a theory, Red." Reggie talks to me, but he shakes
with Digby through his window, hand to wrist as always, as I
dismount the Beast.

"What theory is that?" My limp is pronounced from crouch-
ing through dinner, and I make my way around to where he
stands next to his flashy economy car. It's bright red, like that's
going to make up for the fact that the car is three times too
small for him.

"A girl needs to have some fun after a long, hard coma," he
says. "I mean, comas are so serious. All the doctors, all the near
death."

Digby is still idling in the driveway. I wait for him to turn
off the truck, but he doesn't.

84

"I'm pretty sure my logic is sound," Reggie goes on. "So what do you think?" He nudges me. "Come on, we'll go into Philly. I'm sure someone's playing somewhere divey. Still have your ID?"

I do. Parker, Digby, Reggie, and I paid way too much money for fake IDs last year when Parker's delinquent cousin came into town. Everyone except Lucille, of course. She refuses to break the law. We have to leave town to use them, because everyone knows us here, but whatever. I curve around my own mood, try to make my voice into something pliable and sweet instead of harpie-shrill like it wants to be. This boy stands between me and my bed, and I don't know how to explain to him how dangerous that is.

I think about dinner at Lucille's, about days and days of soon-to-come experiences just like it.

"I'm tired, Reggie," I say. "I need a nap. For, like, twelve hours. We have school tomorrow."

I'm not regular tired. I'm soul tired.

To sleep, perchance to dream . . .

I'm about unconscious right now, on my feet.

"I was up at four-thirty this morning to make practice, dude," he says to me. "And I have to do the same thing tomorrow, too. Coach totally disrespected our vacation. So I don't want to hear your excuses. It's nothing but jibber-jabber."

85

I feel a tug. If I were still me, I would have to get up too for early morning ballet. Life at school would be nothing but the filler connecting the two important parts of my day. The dancing parts.

"You should go with Reggie," Digby says. "Really. Why not?"

"Because I already had an outing. Because I'm not supposed to. I'm supposed to rest. To get ready for my reintegration. So I can fail at something else."

"You're the most rested person I've ever seen," Digby says. "You've been awake for more than a month, but you're still sleepwalking."

"Obeying doctor's orders," I mutter. "They told me to take it easy."

Reggie and Digby communicate over my head, mostly with their eyebrows, like I can't see them, like they're at all subtle. That keeps happening, and it's really starting to piss me off.

"Cut it out!" I yell when I can't take it anymore. "You called Reggie because you're feeling guilty and you want to pawn me off on someone else so you can soothe your conscience," I say to Digby. "You made Reggie come over here, so don't act like I'm stupider than I am."

"Made?" Reggie throws his hands up. "I resent that. I'm my own man. I make my own choices. Made . . ." He opens his door. "Can we go? It's too cold for this. And look!" He points to Parker. "I even put him in the back."

I stare into the car, not moving.

"I have to go back to Lucille's," Digby says, slowly. "To help her clean up." He turns away. "We were going to watch a movie. Or something. I don't think it's good for your head to be spending so much time with that coma girl, or Mom and Dad, or just sleeping. You aren't *doing* anything."

"Breathing," I say.

I have a vicious urge to wrestle Digby from his car and kick him unconscious, but I'm too weak. It would be like trying to beat up a mountain.

"Go back to Lucille." I shoo him. "Go on. Scurry. Watch a movie," I say. "Or help Wrenny with her science fair project, play stepdad, or stepbrother-in-law? Really, Dig, what *are* you? When you figure it out, let me know."

"Harsh," Reggie says.

I begin hacking, like whatever monster has possessed me is trying to climb out of my throat. Reggie pats my back.

"Chill, Red," he says. "This anger is no good for you."

"You're trying to make me feel bad for having a life." Digby's voice is low, head still pointed away from me. "You're jealous."

"You are," I say, even though that makes no sense. What would he be jealous of?

87

"Oh, real mature," he says.

"Digby, you are so close to an ass-kicking right now," I say. "Drive away."

I'm not jealous like he said. That's not the right word.

You went on, I want to say.

Digby sits, arms crossed at his chest. He's such a boy. All you have to do is tell him to do one thing to have him do the other.

"Don't drive off a cliff," I say. "Really."

"The hell is wrong with you?" Dig says, as the car lurches into reverse. *"Really."*

"Hey, hey, now." Reggie opens his passenger door. "No need for uncomfortably hurtful sibling dynamics. Very stressful," he says, and he shoves me into his car.

But gently.

SO THIS IS BEING YOUNG AND ALIVE.

I'm in a club because Reggie said we needed to get out of our comfort zones. I'm nervous to go in, since I've been sensitive to sound and everything, but I know as soon as I'm past the bouncer that I'm going to be fine. The music is a dull throb, not a knife to the ears.

Reggie and Parker are more of the live-band types, like Digby, but I've always preferred clubs, although I've never been to this one. This is usually my comfort zone. The dancing. Disappearing into a world of moves. Music blasts. Bass grinds.

Tonight the place is overfilled and hot, which is nice after the frigid winter weather. But I'm sweating to the point of near suffocation. I feel faint. I should fist-pump, or swing a glow stick, or put my hair in pigtails and slather myself in frosted body butter. I'd probably feel better if I got in the spirit of things.

Reggie and Parker stand on either side of me like bodyguards, making sure I don't get pummeled by anyone in the audience. Everyone looks like they're our age to me, like it's a fake ID summit, and since winter break is almost officially over, everyone who has to go back to high school tomorrow is here.

I knock back my third aquamarine Jell-O shot, which is, as it turns out, my new favorite thing because there's no choking involved. No drowning in my own body. It just slides right down the back of my throat and then settles in my stomach and warms everything.

I let my hips fall from side to side, but they pop, unlubricated. I'm in my tank and jeans and still dripping. The DJ has a mask on, some anime thing with pink hair, and she's good, paying attention to the crowd. She has the right instincts, understands when it's time to drop in the bass, when it's time to tease. There was once a version of me that would have wound up on the stage, straddling the speaker. That version of me is a specter, weaving and gliding between throngs of jiggling torsos. She is having a grand old time while I stand here.

I'm trying to get into the music, to be positive, to move on. I really am. But all I see is cheap glitter and drunk people, some trying to be cool and aloof, others so sloppy their eyes roll back in their heads from the sheer bliss of not giving a fuck.

Therein lies the rub, Eden Jones.

You give lots of fucks.

About Parker's situation, for instance.

"Hey," I yell into his ear, "what's up with the hair?"

"What?" he yells back.

"YOUR REALLY BAD HAIR! WHY ARE YOU DOING THAT TO YOURSELF?"

He pats the bun on his head, strokes his beard, and scowls at me.

"And that's another thing." I point to his chin scraggle. "Consider killing it with fire."

"It's catnip." He takes a defiant chug of his beer. Microbrew, naturally.

"Yeah, I'm sure it is," I say. "For actual cats."

"You know what?" Parker says. "Ever since you had your accident, you're a total bitch."

It stings, but from far away.

"I didn't mean anything. Just trying to help you out. But really," I say, "keep on with your bad self. Lumbersexual is so hot right now."

Reggie steps between us with a new drink for himself and another shot for me.

"Hey, Red, let's get a breather." Reggie leads me through the crowd until we're out on the sidewalk. My ears ring from the noise inside and the sudden relative silence of the alley, and the blessed, yummy cold.

A guy stumbles by, carting a sleeping bag on his back, leading a dog by a rope. He doesn't look at us, and I wonder if maybe he's like the flowers, so slow, so graceful are his movements, so obliging and well paced is the dog. He doesn't look real. He is something I brought back with me, a wandering shadow puppet.

"Did you see that guy?" I say, pointing as he rounds the corner, the dog loping placid alongside.

"What?" Reggie says, standing up straight. "What guy?"

"I have no idea," I say. "Never mind."

Reggie's arm goes around my shoulder, and I grab the shot, slurp it down, and then lean into him. He is a soft place, even though he's made of muscles.

"You can't be like that with Parker," he says. "It's kind of funny, but the boy is sensitive."

"What kind of jock is he? Isn't he supposed to be a modern gladiator or something?"

"The secret poet kind," he says. "With a hell of a repertoire on the court."

"Well, I'm sensitive, too," I say. "To poor fashion choices." I laugh and hit my head on the brick behind me.

"Ouch, Red! Be careful with your noggin."

"Got a smoke?" I say. I haven't really thought about smoking, but now I want one all kinds of bad.

"I am an athlete," Reggie says. "Shame on you for even asking." He rubs the back of my skull. "You would think your injury would keep you from banging your head around. It's serious."

"I'm serious, too. Got scissors? I'm going to go chop that bun right off." I snip in midair.

Then, I don't know why, but I have to rest my head in my hands.

"You all right, Red?" Reggie says. "You holding together?"

His soft jacket rubs against my cheeks, and I think about him when he was four and I asked him to marry me, how he pushed me away and I pinched him. We're only seniors in high school, and it's already been a long road. Reggie read to me in the hospital. I heard him.

I cup his cheek in my hand and then I kiss him, and his lips are soft, but they hang there not doing anything.

"What's up with that?" Reggie says when I pull away, and I can tell he's trying hard not to wipe at his mouth. "Now I know you're having issues."

"I love you, Reg," I say, and I hate how sloshy I sound. "I

want you to know that. Because life is short. I don't ever want you to not know that."

"Okay, glad to see you can still get your buzz on," he says, pushing me away. "And I love you, too, Freakshow. Like a *sister.*"

"Well, you don't have to make it gross." I pull back. "That's crossing the line, sir."

"No, you crossed the line. And it *is* gross." He sips on the fruity vodka drink he stashed under his jacket. This is my favorite thing about Reggie. That he loves sweet drinks, preferably with an umbrella, and a cherry is even better. "You're going to get yourself into a lot of trouble with that 'life is short' stuff if you're not careful, giving yourself permission for nonsensical shenanigans. Like kissing me, because no."

"But I never kissed anyone, ever. Did you know that? Not one time in my whole life."

"What?" He empties his drink. "Drunken Club Confessions, take one. Go!"

I shrug. "I'm pure as the driven snow. It's one hundred percent pathetic."

I throw on my hoodie, finally cooled down.

"Lady, you are eighteen years old," he says. "Explain yourself."

"I'm like a nun of yore." I swing my hips into his. "Married to the dance." I have to insert an accent so it sounds less like something an asshole would say.

"But . . . spin-the-bottle, truth or dare." He's literally pulling on his own hair. "We were such little degenerate kids. That can't be true."

"I wouldn't lie to you," I say.

It's true about the kisses. I always found an excuse to leave when people started falling all over each other, before the parents figured out it was time to put a stop to the coed sleepover parties. And then when everyone was doing it on purpose, kissing and hugging, not in a game, my brother was always involved, or other boys who were like brothers. Either way, I wasn't about to make out with any of them, and the whole thing seemed germy and cesspoolish.

"I never even wanted to. Kiss, I mean. Except in theory. But now I do." I swing both arms around his neck. "Come on, Reggie, let's fall in love." I let my head roll back, pucker for another hooch-smooch.

"Oh, friend," he says. "No. Please hear my words."

"You don't want to be my lover?"

He cackles. I'm being rejected right now. Good thing I can't feel it.

"Okay fine. But I need a reason to stay here, Reggie. Because you should see the other place."

"You don't go deciding to fall in love." He either doesn't hear what I said or chooses to ignore it. "You just do. Falling in love is not something you do with your brain."

"Untrue. Chemicals. Hormones. Pheromones. Love is nothing but science." Judging from the look he's giving me, Reggie must have a secret love somewhere, hiding. "Anyway, I could have died without a single kiss. And now I know I won't. So thank you."

"Sweetheart," Reggie strokes my sweaty forehead, "you're welcome. But listen to me. Love is not science. There's magic in it. Just wait," he croons. "Just you wait."

SOMETIMES BREATHING IS HARD.

It's because I thought about the air going in and out of my lungs, which a person should never do. That's when the act of breathing got awkward, like all things do when you think about them too much. Even your name can sound disturbing and wrong if you dwell on it. So now, because of all the fussing, I've forgotten how to breathe, which I explain to Digby when he meets my eyes in the bathroom mirror from the doorway, where he's stalking me, an almost-empty bowl of cereal and spoon in hand.

"I don't know about breathing. But I do know you can't go to school in that." He indicates my general area.

I shouldn't be going back to school today, nothing to do with my outfit. Not with a hangover on top of everything else. But today it is. I'm not backing down now.

Digby won't maintain eye contact, so I know he's still hurt over everything from last night, but we go on, layering conversation over pain, over regret, over misunderstandings. I take off the robe Sally and Rita gave me so Dig can see that I'm actually dressed underneath.

"You need a belt, or your pants are going to fall down." He stares at my baggy jeans. "And, like, some mascara or something."

"Out." I point for the hallway. The amends I was planning on making, the softness I was striving for, slips away. "Get out of here if you're going to be lame," I say.

He doesn't go anywhere, only scrapes the bowl and eats the very last of his cereal like a cow chewing cud. It crunches at my headachy brain.

"No, really," I say. "Chew louder, by all means. I love it."

No matter how much I mess with my hair, change my pants and shirts, I can't achieve pretty. That's something I didn't always care about, that I didn't even really want. I only thought about being light enough to throw and carry. I miss the part of me that didn't watch the mirror, that stalked mindlessly about like she was going to consume the world.

I've already slathered on several layers of makeup and taken them off again, and am working on my overly blushed cheeks with a cotton ball.

"Put your hair in a ponytail," Digby says unhelpfully, when I start trying to cover the bald spots again. "And let's *go*."

"It's not that easy."

I plop onto the side of the bathtub, so worn out it's hard to imagine there's a whole day ahead of me, that I am at the beginning and not the end.

"It's not so easy going back," I say.

"Oh, come on," Digby says. "It's just till after lunch. Then I'll bring you back and you can crawl back in your hole. We can deal with your feelings later, okay? We'll set aside some quality time and talk them over one by one. Right now, though . . ."

I see myself limping through the halls at school, getting shoved into a wall by Betty Sargent, who always hurts people by accident. Then I get mad at her and yell, and we both go home crying. I see myself dealing with Mr. Liebowitz, who will feel sorry for me but will also be a little mad that I get to waltz back in after being gone for a bunch of school while he's had to grind it out with the riffraff, so he'll be passive-aggressive and stutter when he says my name. I see myself choking on a chicken nugget, on a Tater Tot in the cafeteria. Everyone laughs, even Reggie and Digby and Lucille, because watching someone choke is funny to idiot humans and the natural response to funny things is laughter.

That's when I set the whole school aflame with my powers of telekinesis, because if I'm going down, we're all going down. No one gets out alive.

I let go of my hair, and it falls over my shoulders, a crown of electric copper wire.

"Can I borrow that?" I point to my bald spots.

Digby takes the hat off his own head and puts it on mine.

"We have five minutes," he says. "Don't make me leave without you. I'll do it."

"Dig," I say, "you're making me feel stabby."

"Aw, that's so sweet," he says. "And I'm super intimidated by you. Now get your ass in the truck."

Still, he waits until I'm ready, then hands me my black scarf, which does a perfect job of covering my throat.

I LOST SIX MORE
DAYS OF MY LIFE.

After my attempt at school, which failed, I went so unconscious Mom thought maybe I had fallen back into a coma. This she informs me of as she rips open the curtains in my room.

"Mother," I moan. "Why, though?"

BC is behind her. I hear him wagging his tail into the furniture as he thumps over to say hello to me, resting his head on my pillow millimeters away. I pat his nose and pry my eyelids apart. I have to pull on them with my finger where a thin layer of cement glue has formed.

"It's beautiful outside," Mom says to the blinding white. "The doctor says you have to get up. He says I can't let you sleep like this, no matter how tired you are."

"You called Spock?"

"Spock?"

"He's the one who told me to rest."

"This isn't rest, Eden. This is . . . more coma."

"Low blow," I mumble.

"Honey—"

"Never mind." I throw back the covers. "You could have woken me up."

"We tried, Eden," Mom says. "We tried everything. But you were in an altered state and not your best self."

A flash. Screeching. Throwing a pillow. Tears.

My computer brain is on the fritz again.

I take a careful sip of water while Mom stares outside. My throat scratches.

My bedroom window looks out onto her garden. Mom never had one of her own when we lived in town next door to Lucille. Only a decent patio and a few planters. We've spent one summer in this house, and I woke up every morning to her out there puttering in the early hours, before it got too hot and humid and she had to go to work. I would stand next to her, a cup of bitter black coffee in hand, and listen as she named the flowers she was planting.

Peonies, she would say, *delphiniums, tiger lilies, bee balm, butterfly bush, cosmos, gladiolas, black-eyed Susans, coneflowers, lavender, zinnias, sunflowers, chaste tree, impatiens, dahlias, roses.* They sounded like the universe, the answer to something beyond any question I could think of. I didn't have to go outside to appreciate the flowers, of course. The garden peeked over my windowsill every morning, optimistic and spectacular as a rainbow. But I went out there anyway, to listen to her talk about her plants, about bone meal and compost, because something about flower words on my mother's lips was rich and ripe as the soil itself.

That must be what she sees now as she stares into the bleak emptiness, breath fogging, fingertips trailing the glass. Potential.

"It smells awful in here," she says, finally turning her attention back to me with the same look of concentration and intensity normally reserved for her flowers and especially complicated pastries.

"Thanks," I say, hand on my throat.

My lips hurt again, almost as badly as when I first woke up.

"It smells like sleep and, I don't know . . . when you get up to shower, we should open the windows, let it air out, get the clothes off the floor," Mom says.

I am a flower. I need bone meal and water.

"It's probably forty below outside," I say. "You want to open the window?"

But when I look at my room through her mom lens, I get it. This is not a garden bursting with rainbow love. It's nasty. My floor is covered in shoes, boots, leggings, hoodies, and scarves. Plates and empty shake cups are scattered across my desk. I went on a tear looking for something comfortable to wear to

Parker's party, but the effort to change my clothes, to cover my trach scar—it was too much. And then the thought of getting in the shower, shaving my legs, combing through my hair, it killed the party idea dead. I tried to read, but that didn't work either. I climbed back into the robe Sally and Rita gifted me. It's blue and fuzzy and warm. I gave up on everything. My floor is proof.

Digby tried to get me to rally. I remember that. But he exhaled like he was relieved when I told him I wasn't going.

So go, I thought, and may have said out loud, as he fake-pleaded with me to get up. *Get the hell out and go back to your awesome new life with my best friend.*

But how was that six days ago?

"We'll close the door behind us," Mom says. "That way the cold air won't cost the whole house its heat." She grimaces. "And I'll take care of this mess. It's going to be okay."

She sits at the foot of my bed, and she is even more compact than usual, her hair down, frizzy at the bottom and greasy near the scalp.

"So it's Sunday?" I say. "Again?"

She hands me a glass of water from the bedside table and nods.

More memories jangle through the murky pathways in my brain.

The longest day at school. My locker a shrine of photographs of me. Like I'm dead. Mr. Liebowitz giving me a pep talk about college and my writing skills and applications. My legs like marble blocks, my eyes like lit cigars in my skull.

Home again. Admitting defeat. Days of marathon TV.

My bed.

Getting up to go to the bathroom. To drink water. Then back to the safety of the covers. I wasn't just going under. I was trying to get somewhere just out of reach. To the other place, the one with the peace, where everything was right. Like a magnet I'm half stuck to.

"Have you looked through any of the cards people have sent you?" she says.

I shake my head.

"I thought you might write some thank-you notes. Oh, and look."

She motions to my desk.

"Someone brought a bouquet just yesterday," she says. "You haven't been forgotten."

Two dozen of the most perfect white roses I have ever seen rest in a vase under my shelf of pointe shoes.

I sit upright.

"Who?" There's hysteria in my voice, or maybe it's

excitement. I'm not sure, but it's louder than the room calls for. "Who brought them?"

"What do you mean? The flowers?" She looks perplexed and smoothes the skin on her wrist. "I have no idea. I mean, this kid brought them to the door."

"Kid?"

"Yes, I guess he was around your age. Not that you're a kid," she says. "I know you're an adult now." She sighs. "What a year."

"Was there a card?" I nearly destroy the flowers looking for one.

"The—"

"Card!"

She's blank.

"Mom! Was there a card with the flowers?"

"Wow," she says. "I haven't seen you—"

I finally find it, a little white rectangle, nothing on the outside and plop into my desk chair, nearly out of breath.

"What on earth?" Mom says, a light dawning. "I knew I had seen him somewhere before. The hospital, right? Eden?"

ME AND JAZ WANT YOU TO COME BACK, the note says.

"Eden? Do you know him? Who is he?" Mom says as I flop back onto the bed, card in hand, reading the words again and again. "Is that a grin?"

Flint taps against the granite in me, and before I can tamp it down, there is a spark.

Patient name: Eden Jones

Note: Although patient continues to show improvement, she spends long periods unconscious. She will not discuss it; however, based on information given by her mother, she appears to be experiencing hallucinations as well as persistent exhaustion and alienation coupled with intense emotions, both positive and negative. Her first attempt to return to school was unsuccessful. She has been abusing alcohol, is herself abusive to her family, is refusing to fill out college applications, and may not graduate from high school. Patient is not reintegrating properly at this time.

Conclusion: Patient continues to require close monitoring. Therapy highly recommended.

THIS THERAPIST LOOKS LIKE SHE COULD USE SOME THERAPY RIGHT ABOUT NOW.

"Are you willing to try it?" Dr. Gat says, again.

"Well, Dr. Gat . . ." I begin. I wish so much that I had my leather jacket.

"Marlene," she says. "Please call me Marlene."

"Well, Marlene, I'm not sure why I should."

She smiles, shows me clean, crooked teeth. Her eyes are warm but unreadable, like she went to some special therapist school where they teach you to be both accessible and opaque. She's close to six feet with short brown hair that she's had trimmed into some sort of style but which is more or less a bowl cut. She is decidedly boxy. And nice, I guess, although she's been annoying me since I got here.

I don't know what I'm doing in therapy, except that Mom made it known that she would be investigating new and different circles of hell in which to deposit me (support groups, art classes, tutoring) if I didn't agree to come, so I shall humor them all.

I've never been in a therapist's office, and this urge to scream, to make noise, to disturb things has caught me off-guard. It's how freaking serene it is in here, with the jade plants and the ficus and the water feature and the fish tank. It's also the clothes flowing off of Marlene's enormous frame, like a great wind sail. She does actually resemble a boat of some kind, and she's looking at me like she knows about things in the world (my world), like she knows more about me than I know about myself, when she knows nothing at all about me except what my paranoid, frightened mom has told her.

But it's okay. I can withstand this hour because I have something to do when I get out of here. I saw Joe on my way in, and I am going to bother him as soon as possible. He was at the flower stand, but he didn't acknowledge me at all. I even waved and then, when he didn't wave back, I had to pretend I was stretching. But still. Flowers! He brought me flowers. To my door, twenty-five minutes away from here.

"Eden, what are you thinking about right now?" Dr. Marlene says. "You brightened."

I put the pen and red notebook she gave me down on the coffee table between us.

"Your mother told me you love lists," she says, eyes jumping to the notebook, then back to me.

"Loved," I say.

Once upon a time, there was a girl who had her whole life plotted out in lists. There were short lists and long lists, ones in cursive and illustrated ones, too. They were on pads of paper and napkins, on shoeboxes and toilet paper rolls and sometimes on the soles of her shoes. Lists about wall colors in future apartments and college auditions. Budgets were made, detailing the potential costs of living in New York City. There were graphs. Ambition lists. Organizational lists. Aspirational lists.

Then she fell and hit her head.

The end.

"Before," I say, "I loved lists."

Gobbledygook. Trash. Waste of time.

"You had a five-year plan, yes? Your mother said you always did. Charted everything? Thought your way through each problem, through each next step?"

"Before," I say again.

"But I'm wondering, do you have a plan for your life now? Where do you see yourself in five years? Has your vision for yourself changed?"

Why, yes. Now the plan in five years is to be suffocating on a down comforter.

In my parents' basement.

"Speaking of life," I say, "can we talk about death for a second?"

She leans back.

Defeat.

"Go ahead," she says.

"What do you think happens when you die?"

"Well, I don't know." She puts her mug to the side.

"Do you believe in God? Heaven? Hell? Reincarnation? Eight hundred virgins?"

"I'm not going to . . ." She collects herself, wipes at her chest as though getting rid of crumbs. "Eden, while religious questions are interesting—"

"Existential, not religious. I want to know what you think happens to someone like me when they have been separated from their body for more than a while? I mean, do they . . . did I really come back?"

"See?" she says, thumping a finger on the notebook. "This is exactly what I was talking about."

Ugh.

"What I'm asking you to do," she says, "*all* I'm asking you to do, is take a look around and write down some of the things you love about being alive. It's simple. Let's focus on living."

"How do you even know I'm alive?" I say.

Her face scrunches all the way. "I beg your pardon?"

"Can you prove to me that I'm alive?"

"I . . . I can tell you that I am experiencing my own life and experiencing you as a person who is alive, and so we must both be."

"Flawed logic," I say. "Ever heard of Group Think? You could be dead too, and we could be having a group delusion. Or you could be a product of my subconscious, or a symbol, or a guide—"

"I am not a symbol."

"Maybe I am."

"Eden, do you truly believe you are dead?"

"No, of course not." I laugh because she's making eyes at me like her fingers are on a secret button that attaches directly to the lock on a padded room. I remind myself to act sane, even in therapy where you're supposed to be a little crazy. "I'm just making a point."

I sit up straight. This hour is almost up.

"Which is?"

"Hunh?" I've lost my place.

"What is your point?"

"About what?" I'm scrambling because I truly have no idea what I was talking about.

Her face goes soft and kindly. "You want to talk about life

and death, Eden? Let's talk about it." She crosses her hands over her knees. "It's natural to be confused, to have questions. I don't know if I can answer them, but we can talk through it all."

This couch, a mustard-colored velveteen, is perfect to sleep on. My eyes begin to close.

"Do you want to tell me what you remember of your experience during your coma?"

I shrug.

What would she say if I told her what happened while I was under, or that I want to find out where Vasquez is right now and also what made me come back? That will seem Unhealthy again instead of Moving Forward like everyone wants. I will keep my Unhealthy to myself. And I especially won't tell her about the black flowers blooming hard above her head, spinning shiny like a halo.

"We don't know anything about anything," I say, after a few minutes under her scrutiny. "As humans, I mean. No one knows whether the reality we are experiencing is *reality* reality or if we're just making it up. You can't say with one hundred percent certainty that I ever did wake up. Neither can I. That's all I'm saying." I pause. "It's speculation."

"Well," she says, "I suppose if you go that far, everything is speculation."

If it's all a dream, I can do whatever I want, and the

consequences are irrelevant because nobody is real. I think about sprouting wings and rising from the building. Maybe I can will it. Nothing happens except that flowers glide along the floor and slither up my legs, which is something, but not the something I was hoping for. And what do the flowers mean? That's what I really want to talk about, what I need to discover. They followed me back here, and until I understand why, I can make all the lists in the world. The key is in the flowers, and Marlene can't help me with that.

"It's great to sift through these concepts, these more esoteric experiences, but let's strike a balance here. Before we part ways, I'd like to get back to some of the steps we're going to take toward you getting in touch with your life," Marlene says. "It's natural for coma patients to feel dissociated, depressed. This is an important part of your recovery, Eden. But let's also look forward."

"I'm the opposite of dissociated," I say, and pick a little black nail polish from my cuticles.

"And so," she persists, "for next time, some things to think about, from the past, the present, the future."

"Ugh," I say.

"I understand your twin brother is dating your best friend rather seriously. We can talk about that?"

No we cannot.

"Also," she says, "we could talk about the fact that you are not presently dancing and that has been a large part of your identity, yes?"

Don't scream, Eden. You've worked so hard on healing your throat.

"You really know how to cheer a girl up," I say, finally.

"Just try the list, okay?" she says, with more than a little sigh. "If you don't connect to anything, we'll try something else. Things you love about life. Give it a chance, Eden. You might get something out of it."

Oh, dear Marlene Gat.

"You might connect," she says, mostly to her tea mug and without much hope. "You never know."

WHAT I CONNECT
TO IS A CHAIR.

*I'm selling flowers to hospital cus-*tomers so Joe can grab something to eat. It was as awkward as it sounds. He was desperate enough to hand me his change bag and tell me to be a good person and not steal from him as he ran to the bathroom and then out the front door. His stepmom, he said, got a cold, so he had to mind the flower stand, and his dad was too busy to bring him food like he'd said he would, so Joe was *starving to death.* On the plus side, we never had to talk about the flowers he brought to my house or why I was hovering about. We went straight to him having to pee real bad.

Being Flower Power girl is awesome. People either jump or smile when they see me. They remember they meant to grab some flowers on their way to whichever sick relative's room. They should have been thoughtful, considerate, but they were too upset or too busy. So when they see me, they exhale, their shoulders relax. They come for a bouquet of lilies, some white roses. At least that's what I think would happen. I've only sold one bouquet to a guy with a briefcase, but he looked pretty happy about it. I go back to listening to pop music, even singing along with the hospital sound system. I love that my throat doesn't hurt when I do it.

I stretch my legs, which are sore from the physical therapy that came before the therapy therapy. But when I extend them, I feel muscle beginning to come alive again. I have quads and hamstrings and calves. I have tendons and ligaments. Dr. Patel says because I was an athlete for so long, my body will remember itself faster than other people's. Still, it hurts.

"Thanks," Joe says.

He's a little out of breath and is back holding a paper sack, looking cherry-cheeked from the snowy day outside.

"What did you get?" I ask.

"Peanut chicken," he says. "I'm hungry, and the guy on the corner makes sick noodles."

People hustle by. It's five thirty. When they're out of work, done with school, the hospital is like a bus station. Joe removes the lid from the bowl and takes a bite. After a silence, he says, "I'm going to lose my mind if this keeps playing. It's like they try to murder you with overproduced nonmusic. They make you walk the line."

"How's Vasquez?" I ask, after a pause.

"Who?"

Hello, Eden. He obviously has no idea what you're talking about with your made-up people names.

"Jasmine, I meant," I say. "Jaz."

A woman with a large necklace made of abalone comes over and asks for a bouquet of white daisies. I collect the money while Joe eats.

After she's gone, he says, "She's not doing too good."

"I'm sorry," I say. "That sucks."

This is followed by sloshing noodle noises.

"Is she your girlfriend?" I ask. "I'm just curious."

He drops his fork and watches me for so long I'm on the verge of going all post-coma Eden on him, when a man in a trench coat buys some lilies.

"For my wife," the guy says. "We just had a baby girl. Lila."

"Excellent!" I say. "Many congratulations."

When the guy is gone, Joe says, "I don't know how to explain Jasmine or who she is in my life. Never had to before."

"Oh." I'm not sure that was an answer to my question.

"What about you? You got a guy?" he asks.

I zip up my jacket. "Please," I say. "Have you seen me? I'm patchy."

"Patchy?"

I point, first to my head, then to all of me.

"You don't look patchy to me," he says. "You look like one of those paintings of the ladies with the long red hair."

"Ladies?" I say.

"I don't know," he says. "I don't know what they're called. But they're not patchy."

He goes back to slurping noodles.

Then, "We've been friends a long time, me and Jaz," he says. "We go to school together. None of the teachers like her. None of them like me, either. So we like each other."

I was right about them fighting aliens, I guess.

"Does she have parents?" I ask. "I've never seen anyone in there visiting her except you."

"She was in foster care, but now she lives by herself. *Lived!*" He says it like he's mad at himself. "She has a roommate, though. Next door to me, behind the restaurant. My stepmom's friend Gigi rented her a room."

"And Gigi," I say. "She doesn't come to visit?"

"Gigi never leaves our street," he says. "She's kind of old and has a lot of rules."

"Like not leaving your street?"

"Yeah, like that."

"Well, either way, Jaz is not dead," I say. "You don't have to talk about her in the past tense, like she doesn't exist anymore."

"Yet," he says. "I don't have to talk about her in the past *yet*. I don't want to tell myself lies. I know how it goes, how life is, how people come and go."

In the room the women come and go
Talking of Michelangelo.

I touch his arm before I have the chance to think it through.

"She's got no one but me." He looks out the front door. "And there's nothing I can do for her. I hate this fucking hospital," he says. "It's like a bad joke they make me work here. Nothing good happens in this place."

This is maybe not the perfect time to mention it's currently the only place I feel halfway normal. It seems buzzing, alive, crackling with possibility. Real.

"What about babies? Look how happy that guy was," I offer. "Babies are born in hospitals, and they're good."

"Until they turn into jacked-up adults like everyone else," he says. "Plus there's, like, a fifty-fifty chance they'll turn out to be bullies, sociopaths — or maybe they get OCD or panic disorder. Depression if they're lucky."

"Damn," I say. "That's dark. And that's saying something, coming from me."

He smiles, scrapes the last scallion from his bowl.

"Want to help me make a list?" I say.

"Of what?"

"There's a lot to like about this world," I say.

There's a lot to like about the other one, too.

I take out my red journal.

"Maybe it would cheer you up to make a list of things like that."

I write *white roses* across the top of the empty page. I pause, then add *flower stands* and *noodle bowls* and then add *babies*. "On second thought," I say, "I don't think this is something we can do together. Too private. You should make your own though. Try it."

He eyes my journal suspiciously.

"Not into this earthly incarnation, hunh?" I say.

"I don't know. Sometimes it's all right, but I've been thinking lately, maybe it's not the worst thing if Jasmine stops breathing," Joe says. "For her, I mean. Not for me. Like, what does she have to live for? Sometimes I can make a whole list of reasons. Other times I can't think of a single thing."

I look at my list. It does seem pretty small and sad compared to Jasmine's problems. No parents, no money, no future.

"And to die is different from what any one supposed, and luckier." When you can't think of anything good to say, say something someone else said. That way, you can blame them if they turn out to be wrong.

He puts his bowl to the side.

121

"I mean, that's what Walt Whitman thought, anyway," I say, trailing off.

He watches me until I begin to pick at the ribbons on the stand, the pink tags that say IT'S A GIRL!

"Hey," I say, "do you know how to bowl?"

He grins as flowers shoot up from the ground, bloom up my legs at full speed, and plunge through my belly button.

THEN THERE IS JASMINE.

Joe and I decide that before we can run off together, we should at least say hello to her. We stand side by side in her hospital room a couple of inches apart until Rita brings us an extra chair so we can both sit, which neither of us does. Jasmine is not looking good today. She's thin, pale, and her lips are cracking. Her arm skin hangs loose. It's as though the human part of her is melting away and all that's left is a husk. Still, I would swear she's in the room. I can see her sitting straight up, spinning her legs off the side of her bed. She would rip the feeding tube from her throat. She would say, "The hell?" She would crack her neck, massage her own shoulders, test her jaw a time or two, and stalk out.

She would if she could.

She can't. She's disappearing.

Still, she's beautiful. Not pretty, beautiful. There's a difference.

"What's happening to her?"

I point to Jasmine. Her hands are shriveling like the Wicked Witch's foot in *The Wizard of Oz,* disappearing into her sleeves.

"Happens," Rita says. "Over time. Happened to you. But she's been under longer, so it's getting worse."

I open and close my hand reflexively, test it. So much has changed since I woke up. I have forgotten the cramped stiffness from those first days, how I promised myself to be grateful when I was healthy again, when everything worked, never to take it for granted, any of it.

"It wasn't this bad on you," Rita says, "but it happened. Everybody's different in a coma. We're individuals, even then."

Joe—who has been staring at Jasmine, still as a boulder—jerks and then thrusts the last of the flowers at me, the ones that were left over and which we brought with us. He fishes some quarters out of his pocket, taps them together like castanets, says, "Be right back," and leaves the room.

"It's hard when you don't know what's coming," Rita says. "In life and in death. And you never really do."

Joe returns a few seconds later with a soda and paces the periphery as though he doesn't want to come all the way in, as though he doesn't actually want to be here at all.

"Is she getting better?" I ask. "I mean, is there any sign?"

Rita shakes her head.

"Joseph," she says.

There's a pause, the kind that precedes a deafening sound.

Rita tucks the blanket around Jasmine's legs. "You're going to have to start thinking about what you want to do about her. About Jasmine."

"I know," he says.

"I'll get the doctor so you can discuss options."

"I don't want to talk about it in here." He nods toward the bed. "What if she's listening?"

"Course." Rita squeezes his arm. "Come see me on your way out. We can talk about it then. But don't run off."

"Okay," Joe says. "I get it."

"Touch is the best thing for her," Rita says, "for anyone in pain or injured, but especially for someone in a coma." We remain motionless. "Maybe you ought to pull your chairs closer in."

When Joe doesn't move, I say, "We will."

She makes to leave the room.

"Hey, Rita," I say. "My brother says he's going to burn that robe you gave me. That's how much I wear it."

"Let him know we believe in an eye for an eye around here. He would be messing with the bull." She raises up one cheek in a half smile. It's a half joke too.

She leaves.

"It's a pretty ugly robe," I say.

Joe throws the old flowers into the cream-colored plastic trash bin at Jasmine's bedside. He gets clean water from the bathroom sink to replace the partially evaporated sludge in the clear hourglass vase.

"Sprite." He cracks it open. "Flowers love sweetness. The dahlias lasted forever this year. They have a better relationship to corn syrup than we do." He pours. "At least that's what Norma says."

When he has displayed the flowers as he likes them in the vase, he sits down, but gets restless and finds a wall to lean against instead.

"It's so trippy," he says from the corner. "Her lying there like that. She never stops moving, you know? In life, at least. She's the kind of person you could cut down over and over, and she'd spring right back up."

"I knew she was a badass!" I say, too loudly. "I . . . I was trying to guess about her personality from looking at her."

Joe sinks down to sit.

"I probably have everything wrong." I'm thinking about Lucille or Dig, how I would feel if someone who didn't know them was trying to act like they did, especially if one of them was hurt, if one of them was possibly not going to survive.

There's nowhere for Joe to hide in here, though he looks like he's trying to disappear into the wall. I wish I could give him a blanket. I wish I could be the blanket.

"So what did you think, then?" he says after a few grinding, silent minutes. "About Jaz. About who she is."

"Really?"

"Yeah, I'm curious."

"I thought she looked like someone who's got stuff to do. Someone busy." I see her reaching for me as she sinks and I buoy, her lips moving.

"That's true." He smiles. "She had two different jobs, was pushing to get through school even though she hated it, rebuilt cars on the weekend. She took me to a couple of junkyards to look for carburetors a few weeks ago. Sometimes it's not a bad thing to stare at the wall, you know? It's good to relax. I would tell her, 'Jaz, relax yourself,' but she was always saying, 'I'll sleep when I'm dead' and 'Drive fast, take chances.'" He shakes his head. "She said dumb stuff like that all the time. Like a walking greeting card for messed-up people. Yeah," he says. "She never stopped moving, like I said. Until she did."

This picture of Jasmine, alive, with busy eyes, busy, buzzing hands — it sits between us heavy and loud, massive.

"You know what happened?" he says. "Fucking motorcycle. She's like the poster child for stupid shit. Not even original.

Would have been better if she had fallen off a cliff or something like that. A motorcycle. No helmet. Ripped her face open.

"Idiot," he says to her. "You're a dumb ass, Dumb Ass."

We are silent for a while.

"I also," I say, finally, "thought she looked like she's into music. I imagined her like a DJ or something. Not like now with the computers, but like when there were turntables."

"That's funny." He's still focused on her. "It's kind of true. I guess you can tell a lot just from looking at someone. She'd surprise you, though."

"Like how?"

"I don't know." His shoulders move away from his ears. "That's true that she's all about music. So that's not really surprising. But, like, she's into all kinds."

"Live bands," I say.

Joe really looks at me for the first time since we came in here, and it startles me. Again. It's like he's peering at me all the way from his tailbone, which is firmly attached to the earth. No, that's not right. That is the earth itself.

"You know," he says, "she would be looking for new sounds, but there's nowhere to go around here. Where is she going to find any underground anything?"

I think about the bar Reggie took me to. I wish I could take her there. My head aches.

"She could go to New York or Philly," I say. "There are places."

"I could barely get her to leave town," he says. "I think it's because of being in foster care and everything being all crazy all the time. She liked her room, her jobs, her life, simple like that. We did get into it a few times, though."

"Like, you fought?"

"Yeah, sometimes." He smiles again and two dimples appear, deep and spacious as coin slots.

"What did you fight about?"

He lets his legs fall out in front of him. "She listened to old stuff. Classic rock, Beatles, jazz." He makes a face. "I don't like any of it, but especially the jazz. People going off on their instruments for hours like that. But she got into it. *Really* into it. I told her she was biased and couldn't hear right because it was her name. Nodding her head at me, snapping her fingers like I couldn't hear for myself, like if I could get inside it, I would understand why she liked it so much." He taps his hand against the wall. "I talked some shit about Miles Davis one day. She didn't speak to me for a week."

I laugh.

"It was annoying! She always wanted to control the music. I don't let anyone drive my truck besides me, and I don't like people touching my buttons." He points at his own chest. "My truck. *My* buttons. She's a pain in my ass."

"So you miss her," I say.

Joe's knees and face meet instantly, and he curls up tight as a potato bug. His stomach is clenched under his shirt, and he holds on to his calves.

I walk over to him and duck down. It's not easy for me to squeeze myself into the corner next to him, but I do. I put my arm around his shoulder.

"Do you ever hold her hand?" I say.

He shakes his head. After a minute, he says, "We aren't like that."

"I don't mean like a girlfriend. I mean like a friend. Like a person you touch. Like this." I run a hand down his sleeve, let it rest where his wrist creases.

"No," he says. "I don't do that."

"Touch?"

"Not really," he says. "Not my thing."

In dancing you can't avoid touch. Hands on my inner thighs, holding me up, on my torso, spinning me. Leaning on Lucille, plopping down on Reggie's lap when there are no chairs. Life is touch, right? What would it be like if I avoided it?

"You could read to her," I say.

"She loves my truck," he says. "It's an old Ford my dad has had a long time. Maybe I could read her one of his magazines about car shows and stuff. She might like that."

"Yeah, that could be good," I say. "Something so she knows you're here, like I did. I remember my friend reading to me. My mom."

"Really?" he says.

"Yeah, totally."

"It's not the same as life," he says. "It's not a conversation. I just want to hear her voice."

He almost breaks. Tears hover over his bottom lids.

I want to give him something, some salve to take away his pain as he sits there wishing his friend would bounce out of bed and get back to being her. Even as I think it, vines creep out from under Jasmine's blanket and my breathing gets shallower, my fingertips tingle. The world is veiled in the unknown. Its mystery singes my throat — the thrill of it, the fear.

The next words are out before I have the time to give them proper consideration, to find out whether they're even actually true. "We could try to talk to Jasmine for real," I say.

His face drops into a question mark. The tears recede.

"Maybe it wouldn't work," I say, backpedaling as he stands.

"It might be a stupid idea. I mean, it's definitely a stupid idea."

"Yeah," he says. "Maybe. But explain what you mean anyway."

I think about exactly how to say what I mean as he stares at me expectantly.

"Okay," I say. "Something besides this does exist. I don't know much more than that, but I'm sure about that one thing." I feel like I'm lying, like I'm making up impossible things to be interesting. I force myself to remember exactly what it was like In Between. Which is when I realize what happened while I was under is fading into an impression of an event like every other memory, turning to shadow and breath, into echoes of itself.

Everything but the damn, damn flowers.

"Something does exist. I saw," I repeat, meeting his eyes. I almost tell him that what I saw was Jaz, but I stop myself. "It's . . . a place. Like this but different." I cover my face and talk into my hands. "I'm sorry. I'm not doing a good job of talking about it. It's so weird, you know? Sometimes it feels like I dreamed it. I didn't though."

He pulls my hands away and studies me. There's nothing mocking or unkind about him, only a curiosity, and beneath that, a terrifying hope. I want to kiss him, hold him. I am the master of inappropriate timing and mad thought.

"And you think we can get there to her?" he says, and I snap to. "Be serious now. Don't mess around."

I realize I was expecting him to laugh at me. He has surprised me. And the surprise fortifies me. I suddenly want more than anything to do this, to find Jasmine and talk to her, to take the flowers back there and find out what they are and why they're following me. To find out, finally, what she was saying to me in the water. To make Joe happy. To give him back his friend.

"I can't make any promises, but maybe," I say. "Maybe we can do it. Maybe there's a way."

"Okay, so how would it work?" he says.

"I just thought of it," I say, mind scrambling. "Give me a second."

He holds on to Jasmine's bed rails, watching her face so intently I feel like a voyeur. "Let's take it slow, Eden. What was it like when you were in your coma, the part you remember? Tell me everything."

I recoil like an anemone, like he has stuck his finger into my jelly.

"It was endless." I'm trying to put words to it, but it's hard.

It feels like something that happened in another life. I double face palm again and growl. "I don't know. I was there for weeks, but it seemed like minutes. It was like I was on a loading dock and the scene kept changing."

"And . . ."

"This is a place. A real place. It's a whole other . . ." I search for a word, but the only ones I can find are *dimension, reality, universe.* "It's a whole other thing," I say, finally, irritated with myself.

"Okay, so let's say we do reach her, that something like that is even possible." He looks at me. "Then what?"

"Then we ask her to come back." Obviously. "To wake up. Someone asked me." I'm remembering now. Reggie's voice, my mother's, finally Lucille's. "It worked."

He brightens. "Hunh," he says.

"I have friends," I say, "parents. They care about me. They're why. I can't be totally sure I wouldn't have come back anyway, but she only has you. So maybe you can bring her back. Maybe you're the key, her ruby slippers. You can remind her there's no place like home."

I smile and nudge him, but my thoughts are darker and more honest. Something along the lines of *maybe we're playing a game and all of it is nothing and I don't want to say goodbye to you or her yet and that is all this is.*

"We could try a séance or something," I say. "Maybe we can find a book that will give us the right incantation. We should Google it."

"Is this funny to you?" he says. "Because they're going to pull the plug on her if she doesn't come around. *I'm* going to. I will have to do it."

"No! I didn't mean . . . I'm sorry. I didn't know."

"She's got no insurance," he says. "She's not responding to anything they try. It's me, okay? She made me her next of kin."

"What?" I say. "That's crazy."

"It was the stupidest thing. When she got emancipated, she went to a lawyer. Made me her next of kin, even though . . . Which means I get her shitty Mercedes and her damn jazz if she . . . And I have to decide whether she lives or dies, so I don't have time for flirting or . . . or playing games. Not while she's lying there."

Flirting. It sounds like a butterfly, like a kite, something that's flimsy and floats and is heavily involved with kittens. Something other people do, people not mixed up in matters of life and death. People who flit.

"Can't her roommate, the woman she lives with, be her next of kin? Or, what about the doctor? Can't someone else decide?" It would be too much for me. I would have nightmares. Having my own life in my hands is enough.

"She hated adults. Didn't trust them. She could barely deal with me once I turned eighteen. No. Jaz picked me," he says, softly, shaking his head. "She's got no one, like you said. No. One. Not some old aunt in California, not a grandpa in Peru. So I can't waste time. I don't want to pretend something is real if it's not. I need help. We either try this or we don't. It's either real or it's not."

Joe turns, and I stand next to him.

He takes my hand. "And you. You're either real or you're not."

"I am," I say. "I'm real."

We face Jasmine together. The flowers weave up and down her legs. They plant themselves in her chest and pulse like a beacon.

"You are not dead yet," Joe says to her.

"You're not dead yet," we say together, as we stand over her inert body. "You're not dead yet."

It's kind of like what they have in the movies, really. The darkness, the tunnel, the people you know who already passed standing there in a line waiting to greet you, the whole bit.

You asked if they look human or like light, and my answer to you is yes.

They're both, and they're happy to see you. They embrace you, and they keep you warm, such as you are. So when you want to know if I'm afraid to die now, now that I'm older and that's coming, I have to say yes and no.

I mean, I don't want to die, and you have to say that out loud so the people listening hear you, because you don't want to send mixed messages about your intentions out into the ether.

I want to live as long as I can.

But the truth about why I want to be here is that my husband is still breathtaking. He's a miracle to me more than any tunnels, any white light, and I want all the days I get with him. We never had any kids, you know, so it's us. I don't want to leave him a minute before I have to. Because I don't know about that part. I don't know if I'll ever get to see him again once this bit is over.

So I guess I'm sure about something a lot of people have questions about, but I still have questions. That's a gift, right?

— *Deanna Lovato, 55, retired lawyer*

JOE'S HOUSE IS NOT WHAT I EXPECTED.

Actually, it's not a house at all. It's an apartment above the flower shop, which is on Main Street, a little way from the hospital. The town of Warrenton is broken down into sections: the newer part that cars drive by all day, the one I've been driving through my whole life when we needed paint, or nails, or an extra-big box of Goldfish crackers. Or to get to the hospital, of course, when Digby broke his arm, that time Wrenny had a bad reaction to a sting. That's what I always thought of when I heard the word Warrenton. Endless chains, infinite fast food, waiting rooms.

But behind that, two blocks over, like hidden treasure, there's another part of town, one that feels like a really old TV show. The houses sit in neat rows, cars drive slower, and buildings are compact and clearly state their purpose under their names.

DRY CLEANER.

BAKERY.

JUICE.

ITALIAN RESTAURANT.

FLOWER SHOP.

It's dark, so each building is barred and illuminated by streetlamps and porch lights.

We climb the peeled-paint stairs that lead up the back way, and Joe hands me the screen door to hold back as he fumbles with his keys and lets us in. I can already smell something amazing.

It's been quiet since I convinced Joe we could figure out a way to talk to Jaz and he said okay and invited me back to his house to discuss it, right before Spock came in all his Spock-ishness and pulled Joe into the hallway to discuss options for Jasmine. I eavesdropped hard but only heard bits and pieces. Enough to gather that Jasmine is fading, that her cerebral cortex is shutting down, that soon, even if she woke up, she would be a vegetable, half a person. They want Joe to sign papers for her peace, and he won't. Not yet.

I wondered if those conversations were had about me, if my family considered removing the feeding tube, unhooking the ventilators, whether they whispered in hallways where nurses and doctors patted their backs and looked at them with fatigued, resigned eyes, and I feel, not for the first time, the weight of it, of the time passed and missed exactly like a river current.

Time is virulent. And it passed right through me as it is passing through Jasmine now, disassembling her as it goes.

Joe and I didn't speak as we stood in the elevator, or when he opened the door for me to climb into his big army green truck, or when he walked around and opened the door for me again after parallel parking into a tiny space like a total superhero.

It's not just him, the not talking. It's me, too. Because on the way here, thoughts about other, more flitty, flirty things floated in. I don't want him to admonish me again, and if I open my mouth, I'll throw everything up like rainbow-colored vomit butterflies, and he'll never want to hang out with me again.

That is something I don't want. Very badly I don't want it. I don't know why, but Joe feels like substance in a cardboard world.

So I will not say:

Why did you bring flowers to my house?

Did you miss me?

Did you meet my mother?

Did she tip you?

We're mute until we're through Joe's front door, because one of us might bolt if there's a sound.

"We're staring at each other self-consciously," I say.

"You like to say embarrassing stuff, I guess."

"Oh, but it could be so much worse. I always say the least embarrassing thing I can think of in a potentially embarrassing situation."

"Thanks for clearing that up. I feel better now." He takes off his jacket and hangs it on a hook, then puts a hand out for mine. "About the self-conscious staring."

It's like everything he says makes me blush. Gross.

"Joseph!" The female voice is louder than necessary, and we both jump.

"Hi, Norma!" he shouts back as he takes off his shoes. "Can you?" he says, pointing to my feet. "She's a psycho about her floors."

My mom, too. She even keeps socks in a basket by the door in case barefoot guests want them. I don't tell him that. I take off my Chucks.

The entryway is cramped, packed with boxes and grocery bags filled with clothes and seeds. A stack of *Country Gardens* magazines sits in a corner. "Pretty as a Peony," reads the headline. Spring will come. My mother's garden. Soon, everything will bloom.

The ceiling beams are exposed and rotted in places.

"Dinner's in twenty minutes." The voice is attached to the lobby flower woman from the hospital. Norma is Brillo hair, dyed what I think is supposed to be red but is actually pinkish.

Egg-shaped head, olive skin, thin lips, and she's covered in a flannel shirt like the ones Joe always wears and a pair of baggy khakis. Finally, white ankle socks with those dangly cotton-ball pompom things on the heels. She's holding tissues, her nose flaking and red around the nostrils, but she has the most remarkably gorgeous eyes the exact color of my jade earrings.

"I ate," Joe says. "But I'll eat again."

"Hello," I say. "I'm Eden."

I extend my hand. She looks at it for long enough that I start to drop it back to my side, but then she rescues me from midair and shakes so firmly that I feel limp and powerless.

"You took your shoes off?" She snags a pack of cigarettes and a yellow lighter from her front pocket and puts a smoke in her mouth. She lets in a blast of air as she goes out, slipping her feet into a pair of work boots as she goes. "Good."

In the kitchen, Joe takes lids off pots and sniffs. One is filled with pungent yellow rice with peas and cinnamon sticks, and one with some yellow curry-type thing in it. The house is overly warm, ovenlike, and Joe, after pulling his sweater off, positions himself across from me and is staring at me like he's watching an animal at the zoo. I try to keep my eyes on him, but they leap everywhere.

My phone buzzes with the urgent SOS ring I've assigned

to Mom, to Dad, to Digby, to Lucille. Mom will be cooking at home. She'll be wondering where I am, I bet. She likes all her ducks in a row, all her ducks where she can find them. Digby will worry, too. I put my phone on airplane mode so I don't have to try to ignore the texts popping up on my screen. I don't want to see them. I don't want to care about my friends and family or their feelings. Not right now.

"Norma's mom was Indian," Joe says. "Aditi. She used to live with us, but she died last year. So Norma makes a lot of this kind of food. Adi used to say it was a big deal for Norma to learn how to make full Punjabi dinner when she was a kid. But what's in that pot is called kitchari. She makes it when she has a cold. It's basically rice and beans."

This apartment is roughly the size of a dinner napkin. It would be perfect for one person, maybe two, but four? "How did you fit so many people in here?"

"There are three bedrooms," he says, looking around. "I guess this place is small, hunh?"

"I didn't mean it like that." It's just that, compared to my house . . . I glance around at the elephants, the colorful pillows on the couch, the pictures on the wall, and the flowers, of course. "Norma isn't an Indian name, is it?"

"Her dad was Italian."

"And you?"

He shrugs. "I'm a mix."

"That's more interesting than me. I'm pure Irish American," I say, pointing to my hair.

"Like my mom," he says. "She was Irish. Red hair. No freckles, though."

"My mom calls those daywalkers, like they're daytime vampires or something," I say. "That's so lucky. I have so many freckles I practically am a freckle. My brother's freckles are better . . . more impactful."

"I love freckles," he says. "Your . . . you have nice freckles."

My body heat elevates again.

"Freckles," he says. "It's the perfect nickname for you."

"Don't," I say.

"I'm going to," he says.

Glancing around, I see pictures of a friendly-looking man with dark hair. He has a bulbous nose and is partly bald, but otherwise seems like a thicker version of Joe. I see Norma, going from young to old, and another woman with long white hair.

"Where is your mom?" I ask.

He shrugs.

I open the pot and inhale the scent of the stew.

"Does she use cream in this?" I say.

He shrugs. "Broth, I think."

A striped cat rips across the room, followed closely by a calico one. "Romeo! Kali! Stop it!" Joe yells as they both leap for the curtains and slide down. "They run a circuit of destruction like it's their job."

"Joe," I say, more focused this time, "where's your mom?"

"She's dead," he says simply, not even looking up from his stirring.

He continues going in circles with the wooden spoon.

"She died of ovarian cancer," he says. "I was eight."

"Joe." I hold his hand. Tight. Everything that comes to mind sounds like a crappy greeting card.

"She was at that hospital until they decided to send her home," he says. "To die. We got a couple last days."

"Yeah," I say, because there's nothing else.

"Yeah," he says. "So that was not good."

"I'm sorry."

"There are a lot of ways to die." He breaks away from me, taking a step back. "I'm finding out new ones every day, working in that place. The lobby makes it look so sweet with the flowers and gift shop. But it's a lie. That is a house of death. It's like some cosmic joke that I work there."

There are more things in heaven and earth, Horatio,
than are dreamt of in your philosophy.

145

Shakespeare.

I can't say it out loud.

I go to the window. I want to look out, to see something beyond this bright, colorful living room that seems to be shrinking, like we're in a pink mouth that's about to close and swallow, and disappear us.

"Jasmine worked there?" Joe said she worked next door, so I point to the restaurant he was probably talking about, watch the courtyard, the garbage cans full of plastic and metal, the grease trap, the flying bits of paper. He is behind me, so close to me that if I leaned back even a little, I would cave into his chest.

"Yeah. She would sneak over here sometimes on her breaks, smoke with Norma, watch a few minutes of TV."

He redirects my arm with his. "And there." He points down into his backyard. "That's the hothouse. For the flowers. A lot of people order theirs, but Norma likes to do as much growing as she can herself. We all kind of do what we can, I guess."

I wonder what Mom would do if I showed up at Crazy Cakes and offered to work, or if I told my dad I'd answer phones or sort his blueprints for him or whatever. They'd probably hurl or faint. Anyway, I've never had time. I've been busy. Digby, too, with basketball and whichever girl. We've all been so busy.

I face Joe, and we are awfully near. I could close the gap without even moving an inch. One of the cats twists and weaves between our shins. I don't look to see which one until Joe breaks away and grabs for a golf ball on the counter, rolls it around the palm of his hand.

"You play golf?" I say.

"No, my dad wishes he did."

He drops the ball and sits next to me. His shoulder rubs against mine. Black buds strain against his skin, which burns. Those are real. I think.

He throws the ball up high and catches it.

"So what do you think?" he says. "What's the verdict? Would you have been better off dead?"

"Trick question," I say.

"Is not. I really want to know."

"I didn't have a choice," I say. "I lived that time. It's what happened."

"But you do have a choice now," he says, continuing with the ball. "We all do, right? You could hang yourself, take pills, throw yourself off a building. Like I said, there's lots of ways to die."

I consider this, and as I do, the blood seems to leave all my extremities, to travel toward the base of my throat. If Marlene Gat had asked me if I thought I was better off dead, I probably would have given her the emo answer. Now I feel like I have to defend something.

"Pills make me puke, so they'd never stay down," I say. "There are no buildings tall enough to jump off and do anything more than break an arm in this town, and I've heard you soil your pants when you hang yourself. And also," I say, "thanks for the suggestions."

"You know what I mean."

"Yeah, I know what you mean, and I don't know why I'm here," I say. "Alive. I just am."

"Okay," he says. "So what now? How do we get to Jasmine?"

"Can I ask you something?" I say.

"Sure."

"Why do you want to get to her?"

He puts the golf ball down and tucks a strand of hair behind my ear. "Because I need her to come back. I need someone to live."

"Okay, but what if she doesn't? I mean, what if it doesn't work? What if nothing works?"

He pauses and seems to give this real thought.

"Then the world is nothing but hurt," he says. For a second, I think he's going to chuck the ball across the room into the wall, but then he throws it into the air and catches it again. "You asked if she was my girl before. I couldn't answer you because even though she isn't my girlfriend, she's totally my girl. She's my one great thing. Do you get that?"

I nod, but that's when I have the worst, most selfish thought I have ever had. *But what about me? I lived. I could be a great thing, too.* I am teeming with jealousy and I hate it.

"So?" he says. "Any amazing ideas about how to get in touch with her?"

"I don't know," I say. "I wish there was a phone for this. Maybe there's an app. Got any closets with doors in the back? Beds covering trapdoors?" Before he can admonish me I say, "I know, I know. This is serious."

"What about a séance, like you said?"

I watch him for signs of a joke and find none. From everything I've seen, he's stable, if a little morose. He seems like the guy who would scoff at anything unearthly, not propose we sit around a table with a Ouija board. But he's desperate. I can see it in the constant flex of his hand, the tension in his mouth. He would do anything for his friend. For Jaz.

"We need a witch," I say. "Or, not a witch. But someone we can talk to. A psychic or something, one who isn't a fake, wherever you find a person like that."

New Orleans, from what I've heard, and that's a long way from here.

Joe's look intensifies even further. "I might know a witch," he says.

"Seriously?" I say.

149

"I don't know," Joe says, making two bowls of mushy, delicious smelling food. He hands me one with a spoon.

"Won't Norma be mad if we eat?"

"No," Joe says. "She'll be fine. Plus I'm still hungry."

We each take a bite and groan. It is so good.

"So," I say after we've eaten for a while. "You were saying some insane thing about a witch?"

He reddens. "When I was little, she made love potions for people in the neighborhood and stuff. Then she got a poltergeist out of Paisanos."

"Do tell," I say. "A poltergeist?"

Joe smiles. "I know it sounds nuts, but I remember all the doors slamming at once when she said some stuff in another language. Had candles lit. It could have been a trick, but I don't know how or why she would do that. Anyway, she believes in all of it. And she's a trip and has books and . . . You'd have to see it . . . her, to get it."

"Next door," Norma says from where she's been watching us for I don't know how long. "What're you waiting for? Jaz in the hospital is no good for anyone." She makes a scooting motion with her hands. "Joseph, you two go talk to Gigi. Now."

GIGI DOESN'T DO COMAS.

"Do you not think if I had these pretend powers you have made up, I would have already done it myself? If I could wake her? You think I would not?"

She says this in a heavily accented scratchy voice, after a few minutes of sitting in her kitchen observing us like we're bugs on an entomologist's mounting board. She was in the process of eating a simple dinner of bread and steamed vegetables and playing some sort of game involving farm animals on a huge smartphone, which now sits to the side.

Her apartment is covered in owls. Owls on the pillows, the walls, the saltshakers, an apron, her plates, the mug from which she drinks her coffee. There are stuffed owls, carved wooden owls, a picture of an owl crashing through glass.

Joe told me, on our way over here, that Gigi is how he met Jasmine. She cooked at the restaurant where Jasmine worked as a busser from when she was twelve, and Gigi finally got fired because she refused to retire and she's, like, a hundred billion years old. Gigi's still mad about that. She is also best friends with Norma when they aren't fighting, which they usually are. Like now. Joe said they got into an argument over lotto numbers and haven't talked to each other in a month.

Gigi has the world's most complex messy bun. It's black and made of dreadlocks and is so massive her hair must go to her butt when it's down. She is about four foot ten standing up to her full height. She sounds French, but Joe has already explained that she's prickly about the French part, because she's Creole from Martinique, which is an island in the French Caribbean where they grow sugar cane and coconuts. Also rum. They really like rum in Martinique.

After she tells us she can't help, even for Jasmine, she punctuates her statement by dropping a sugar cube into a shot glass, then douses it in rum, throws in a little seltzer water, squeezes in some lemon, and covers it with a red-and-white-checkered napkin she tells me she stole from "that piece-of-*sheet* restaurant across the street." After handing the glass over to me, she throws her hands on her hips and stares while she waits. This is supposed to be some kind of consolation, I think, or maybe a test, so I drink it.

It is a delicious, sweet burn.

She makes another for Joe.

"No," he says, waving it away. "No thanks."

She drops it down her own throat.

I have the feeling that we could vanish into a closet full of taxidermied animals and never be seen or heard from again. I wonder how I would look stuffed. I also wonder about Jasmine's room, which must be down the hall. I see no pictures of her, no evidence that she is a part of this household, and although I'm curious and hoping Joe will take me to her room, I don't dare to ask.

"Where Jasmine is," Gigi says, "you can think of it like this: you are walking down a hallway, holding a piece of string. When someone else touches the string, you feel it, even though the person is at a different point of contact and you don't necessarily know that is what is causing the disruption."

I see Jasmine, wandering, dressed in white gauze. She's luminous. She holds a glowing white thread.

"It's simpler than you think," Gigi says, "and more complex. But it is not something we can touch from here, even those of us with an interest in such things."

Plus, no one wears gauze, least of all Vasquez.

This morning the only things that mattered were Lucille, Digby, my messy life, college applications, dance, my legs, my limp, my throat. And now I've ventured into a land of curry and extremely attractive boys, and strings in impossible hallways.

"Gigi, do you still play your cards?" Joe says.

She makes a small *pffth* noise and pulls a deck of what looks like regular playing cards from her apron. They're tattered and worn, some splitting themselves apart.

"*Chéri*," she says, "of course."

"Will you choose one for Jasmine? Maybe it can give me a hint about what to do," Joe says, and I'm momentarily paralyzed by how much this makes me feel for him. He's really willing to try anything, to believe in anything. And he's different than I thought. Better. This is a bad time again, but I want to slam him against a wall and kiss him really hard. Something is seriously wrong with me.

Just you wait . . .

Reggie's voice echoes.

No, Reggie. Not that. Not right now. Rain check?

Joe, stop being adorable immediately.

Gigi picks up her plate of carrots, takes it to her small dining table.

"In my experience," she says, "the universe doesn't answer questions so much as it likes to ask them. But you go ahead. You choose one." She points with a knotty hand, shuffles, turns the cards over in her hands, and fans them out. "Pick. Go on."

154

He lets his fingers float over the cards as she smiles at him. Her giant glasses slip down her nose. He picks. Nine of hearts.

Gigi beams.

"What does it mean?" he says.

"It means," she says, "that you should take your friend and go somewhere nice."

Joe shifts around like his chair is molten.

"Gigi," he says, refocusing, "will you please try, try to see if there's anything that can help Jasmine? Anything?"

She purses her lips and worries her fingers across the table and back.

"Come on," he says. "You're all she has besides me. You have to. Even if you fail."

"Tell me one thing," she says. "Why do you concern yourself about the dying when you have the living here?"

She sweeps in my direction.

"Never mind," he says. "I thought you cared about her too, at least a little." He stands and nods his head in my direction. "And she can't replace Jaz. Is that what you're saying? Because that's messed up and I barely even know her."

Umm. I'm right here.

"One has nothing to do with the other," Gigi says. "Jasmine is a child I have housed and fed. Of course I care about her. But we all die. You are . . ." She looks up as though to find a word

155

in midair. "You are conflating my love and the laws of the universe. That's it."

"What does that mean?"

"It means I will think about this whole debacle and determine the correct approach. Without you and your belligerence." She squeezes his cheek. "I know you mean well, Joseph, but if I'm to contact her, even to try, I will need time. Which means you will need to get out."

"Okay," Joe says. "But . . . it's Jasmine. Don't forget."

"*Non, puce,*" she says. "*Bien sûr que non.*"

I wish I could ease his worry, tell him that not having a body is like being in a corset your whole life and finally having it loosened. But he doesn't want her free. He wants her here.

"She doesn't have much . . . or I don't have much," he says. "I don't have much time left."

"Joseph," she says.

"But if we can help . . ." Joe says with a sigh.

"Grieving royals would relinquish kingdoms for five more minutes with a loved one," she says. "I am not a god. I'm an old lady who plays with herbs and cards. What makes you think whatever is out there even has the power to help her, and if it does, why is it going to listen to me?" She pours herself another rum and drinks.

"We have to try," Joe says. "What could it hurt?"

My hand is in Joe's in an instant, and I hold on tight.

She looks at us, stabs a carrot, and then drops her fork down after touching it to her lips. It clatters and tumbles to the side.

"Okay! Fine!" she says. "But you know when I was little on the island, I saw zombies, and I tell you when it comes to life and death, one must be careful. I am doing this against my will for you little terrors. You are lucky you are so adorable, Joseph."

Adorable. That's exactly what *I* think. I like Gigi even better now.

She rubs her hands together as though washing them of the whole thing.

Joe and I both sit down at the table, fingers entwined. His get so tight on mine I have to see what's happening on his profile. Intensity, that's what. Every feature forward.

"I will see what she will show me." She closes her eyes. "If anything."

Joe's palm dampens against my own, or maybe that's mine against his. I wish for water. Cars go by outside; someone yells something in Italian. A dog barks. Above all there's breathing. Mine, Joe's, Gigi's. It's so loud and concentrated that I feel it in my whole body. There are flowers behind my lids. White ones. Black ones. They rotate and spin.

Gigi exhales, and when I open my eyes, she is staring right at me. She pushes at her glasses.

"I have found Jasmine," she says.

"Really?" Joe finally lets go of my hand, but he leaves finger-prints.

"She doesn't know what is happening," Gigi says. "She is in a state of confusion. She is liminal. You know this word?"

"In Between," I say.

"She's in the lining," Gigi says, nodding. "In neither place. And I saw someone else there as well. She was not alone."

"Who?" says Joe. I am certain he is hoping she will say she has seen his mother, that he is wishing for the five minutes to topple kingdoms Gigi mentioned.

"I saw you."

She's talking to me, and I'm as startled as if she has slapped me.

"Eden?" Joe's voice is somewhere between fear and accusation.

"Jasmine doesn't know she's here, and you don't know you're there."

My skin tightens over my entire body like shrink-wrap.

"And you are the only one she can talk to," Gigi finishes.

"Me?" I say. "Why me?"

"Because you are there. You are the only one." She drives a fingertip into my chest. "You."

I SHOULD BE FLIPPING OUT RIGHT NOW.

But I'm not. The night is almost over, and I'm in the Beast, taking notes in my driveway. I scribble in the journal. Because I found more things I like about the world and want to remember what and how much.

Some examples:

* elephants
* owls
* windows
* playing cards that aren't playing cards
* mysteries

I make a new column. For things I used to like.

* dance (the prospect of fame)
* college (conceptually)
* living at home (because I didn't know any different)

159

I put the journal away in my bag, my head still buzzing with Joe.

We never went back to his house after Gigi's because of what Gigi had said to me about me being with Jasmine in a place I've already been. It freaked me out so badly, Joe took me to Digby's car at the hospital parking lot, and we sat in his truck and talked until I felt normal enough to drive, and that's when all the bad feelings went away and everything got totally awesome and Joe told me about himself.

- He likes fantasy novels of the Piers Anthony variety, with centaurs and Pegasus and sexy cyborgs.
- He likes country music and seafood and the feel of dirt on his fingers but not underneath his fingernails, so he always carries a Swiss Army knife so he can get it out.
- He hates school, always has, but has applied to a couple of state schools anyway, because his dad made him.
- He hates not having friends, not caring about the same things other people do. Getting a job, making money, raising a family — none of it makes sense to him.
- He wants to visit every wonder, and learn to fit everything he needs into an army bag so he's free to go anywhere, anytime. He wants to travel the world, to see what's out there.

- He would be an astronaut, except he can't because of the math involved, but he suspects space is the coolest place there is with all that silence, all those stars, so much less gravity.

That's a list, a good one.

He told me about a telescope that is going to be ready soon, that with it we'll be able to see so much more of space it will make what we've seen so far seem like two-dimensional black-and-white.

Eventually, I talked too. About what it was like to dance, how I had dreams of flying since before I can properly remember and that the first time I did a pas de deux and Leo Antonopoulis carried me high above his head, I felt like I was in those dreams, like I had returned to something important, not that I was doing it for the first time. But how I never really found friends in ballet either, how I was too focused on my work, and how I think sometimes people thought I was mean.

"So are you mean?" he said.

"No!" I think about the times other dancers had asked me over to birthday parties and later just party parties, and how I had never even considered it. "Not on purpose," I said to Joe. "I was social . . ." I paused. "With my three friends." It sounded so terrible. "I was focused," I tried again, willing him to understand me. I stared at Joe in the starlight. "I guess I have been a bitch on occasion, even though I never meant to. It seems like you have to, or people take advantage."

"Yeah," he said. "I get it, for sure."

"People either enslave or are enslaved. Starts on the playground with who gets the good swing, who gets to go first on the monkey bars, and it keeps on from there."

"Yeah," he said. "I read *Lord of the Flies* for school. That's what you mean, right?"

"Exactly," I said. "I never wanted to rule anyone, and I definitely didn't want anyone messing with me, enslaving me."

"It's like that, even in a house on the hill?" he said. "I pictured it like everyone happy with their appliances and lawns."

"Nah. People are the same everywhere," I said. "It's basic."

"So you always kept yourself like you do now, with the hood and everything?"

I pulled the hood off my head.

"I'm trying not to scare anyone with my scars."

He ran a finger over the bald spots and smiled. "It's soft. Like duck feathers."

"And there's this." I pulled off my scarf, slowly, exposing the serrated, sawed-up-looking skin that puckered at my throat. I didn't say ugly, but I thought it.

"Does it hurt?" he said.

"Only because I was always vain," I said, hating the threatening tears. Stupid feelings. "The hollow of my throat was my favorite part of my whole body. Now it's ruined."

"It's not," he said. "I like it. You look hardcore. Like a fighter. Like you could take me out."

He pulled at my sleeve until my hand was on his leg, and then he left it there and continued to play with my jacket. My throat dried out, and I couldn't talk anymore, plus we had to keep turning his truck on and off to get warm and then cool again. Finally, he climbed down and opened my door for me.

"You going to be okay now, Freckles?" he said.

"Sure." But as soon as he asked me the question, my adrenaline spiked.

"You have to take everything Gigi says with a grain of salt, you know. She's probably just some crazy old lady. I'm sure I hallucinated the doors slamming shut at Paisanos. I was only seven. And Mr. Jace probably fell in love with Miss Elba by himself. I'm sure Gigi's potion didn't do anything."

"Thanks, that's super helpful," I said.

"We don't have to do any of this if it's scaring you."

"I'm not scared," I said, even though I was.

"I'm just saying, I think I got a little nuts thinking I could talk to Jaz and you could make it happen, but I don't want you to get hurt or anything like that. And anyway, like I said, maybe it's all bullshit."

"Yeah, but she knew."

I didn't have to say the rest. We'd already been over it. Gigi knew I had been in a coma. She knew Jasmine and I had been in the same place. She knew too much to shake off, and Joe swore he never said anything to her.

"A couple months ago, I would have thought both of you were either stupid or crazy," I said.

"I am crazy," he said. "Lock me up. I've also seen Santa. I swear I did, so seriously, and you know what they say about memory —"

"Shut up and let me finish." I took a breath. "I *would* have. Before. I don't anymore. Think you're crazy. That's what I mean. Everything has changed."

"Fast, right?" he said. "Things change so fast."

I took hold of his shirt, the little white buttons.

"Joe, I've been seeing things," I said, "since I got back. I haven't told anyone about it."

"Damn," he said, the humor dropping from his face. "Like what? Ghosts or something?"

"Maybe. I don't know. I keep feeling like maybe I'm the ghost, like I'm falling all the time and I'm never going to land."

"Like jumping out of a plane. Feels like you're falling for-ever."

"You've done that?" I asked.

"Yeah," he said. "I love it. My dad's friend Brad owns a lit-tle company. They do runs every day out in Rosecrest by the fields."

"Flying," I said. Being weightless.

He ran a finger down my cheek. Shook his head. "You're not a ghost, you know. Too warm."

I was warm. Very warm.

"I have to go." I needed to get away from him because he was sucking me in.

"Bye for now." He kissed my cheek as I climbed into Beast.

"Okay." I felt suspiciously glowy.

"Man," he said, "I'm sorry."

"For what?" I said.

"For my shitty timing. For kissing."

"It was my cheek."

"Still kissing. Lips on flesh."

"You make it sound so smutty. It's just a cheek."

He leaned in and kissed me then, not on the cheek, and it went all the way to my toes, which tingled like falling asleep.

"Sorry," he said, mouth still against my lips.

And it's there, in that conversation, those parking lot

minutes with Joe, that I am stuck in a loop. Over and over, he tells me he can't kiss me. Over and over, he does it anyway.

I don't want to be an apology.

My toes are still tingly.

Mom and Dad are in the kitchen, waiting. They're positioned around the table like they're waiting for news. Bad news. They know nothing about what's going on with me or about who I am right now. They're almost strangers. Mom has her head down like she's fallen asleep but looks up as BC pops into view at the window, wagging his tail behind him.

Did I really think they would go to sleep not knowing whether I was home? I didn't, because I didn't think at all.

"YOU STOLE MY CAR!"

I blink several times to bring my family into focus, because they're hazy, as though they're in the process of being teleported into the kitchen and haven't completely materialized. I orient myself, or try anyway. My house is made up of the same creamy leather as before, the same plush rugs, hardwood floors. Everything is neutral. The same redheaded, slender mother is before me, the same worn-out Ken-doll dad. Digby, though, is the nearly unrecognizable hue of a beet and carrot salad. My parents are behind him in their matching striped pajamas.

"Beast is right outside," I say. "Safe and sound. Totally not stolen."

"It's *midnight*," he says.

The moment he says it, I sink into a kitchen chair. My legs throb, and my eyelids get heavy.

"Yeah," I say. "I guess it is."

"I have practice at *zero* o'clock in the morning."

"You have practice on a Saturday?"

"I have practice always."

"I had no way of knowing that."

He retrieves his phone and shakes it in my face. "See this?" he says. "It's called a cellular phone. With it you can do all sorts of things such as play games, catch up on social media, and check your damn text messages!"

"Well, I didn't see you getting all psychotic when I was with Reggie. Why weren't you worried about me then?"

"Because Reggie is Reggie. We knew where you were. And I needed my car, Eden. My car."

"You have Lucille's. I saw it in the driveway."

"Yeah, but what if it broke down?"

"You're trying to control me and it's stupid," I say. "You're being so totally stupid."

There's nothing Digby hates more than being called stupid. He has a dumb jock complex. It's low and I know it, but I went an entire evening without feeling tired, without having trouble swallowing, without walking funny. I saw new things. I smelled new things, too. I met a witch. It was cool, and I'm not sorry about that.

Digby is staring at me like I'm a toad.

Mom gets between us and hands me a chocolate shake in a

box. "Have you eaten?" she says. "You look hungry or low blood sugar or something."

I break from Digby's hate stare and take the shake from her so I don't have to explain where I had my dinner. "Thanks, Mom."

"You said you'd be gone a couple hours when you took the Beast. That's all I'm saying, okay? It has been *eight* hours. Eight hours is four times a couple of hours. Lucille was worried. We were all worried."

"Okay," I say, "I get it. But I wanted to be alone for a while."

"It's dangerous," he says. "You acting like this right now while you're still . . . You're the one who's being stupid, not me."

Digby and I have never fought this way. This is because of his relationship with Lucille. Or because I can't be the way I used to be. Whatever it is, I don't like it. I don't want to fight with him, and I can't stop it.

"You're not my mother," I say. "She is."

"Eden." Mom slumps into Dad.

"Give me the keys," Digby says.

I hand them over.

"I don't have to share my car with you."

"Actually," Dad says, "you do have to share it. We had an agreement about Eden and the hospital, Digby. She needs it for physical therapy. When she moves to New York, she won't need one, so there's no point in making the investment now." He stops himself. "At least not yet. We have to see what happens. With her future."

Stutter, stammer, Dad. He runs water into the kettle and turns on the stove.

New York.

College.

Auditions.

Applications.

Say those words out loud. They're like knives, making julienned vegetables of my life.

"Madame called today." Mom says. "Again. She says she's tried you directly a number of times and that you aren't calling back."

When I think about calling her, it's like there's a pane of glass between me and the phone. I see her trying to reach me but I don't know how to get to her without breaking something.

"Do you remember the time you ran away?" Mom's arms are crossed over her chest.

"I've told you I'm sorry so many times—"

"That's not what I mean," Mom says. "Where did you go when you left us? Think about it. Eden. You owe her a phone call, at least."

But I'm damaged. What could Madame want from me as a damaged, useless, scarred-up thing?

"If you take Beast again," Digby says, resuming his dickness, "you are only allowed to go to the hospital and back, not have a mental breakdown and go searching for yourself for days or whatever it is you're doing."

"*Allowed?*" I stand up. I wish I was in heels so I could stare right into his eyes, because this he needs to get really clear about. "I'm not allowed? You think you are in charge?"

"I think I'm in charge of my own car. Yes I do," he says. "And I don't feel right about you driving it. I mean, look at you."

I do. I'm in gray sweats, a black top, Chucks. I have dog and cat hair all over me and a smudge where some food fell on my chest. I shudder to think what my face looks like. Whatever Joe saw in me is wiped away, replaced with nothing but complicated gashes and bruises. Scar tissue.

"You're an ass," I tell him.

"Well, I hope you're on drugs because if not, you're just crazy."

I laugh, a honking sound that changes to a sob, then flips back to laughter.

The kettle whistles.

"Digby, go take a break," Dad says.

I turn off the burner.

"You're sending me to my room? For real?"

Digby crosses his arms and raises his eyebrows. That's what Dad has always said when one of us was doing something wrong, and we're suddenly both giggling. Our parents have never looked more confused.

"I'm fine. You can all relax. Right now, okay?" I hold up the shake. "Thanks, Mom." I turn to Digby. "And don't worry. I'll take the bus Monday. You can keep your car."

"Bus to where?" Digby says.

"Oh yeah. I've decided I'm going back to school." Just now I decided.

The room gets quiet, except for BC's nervous pacing, the click of his nails on the kitchen tile, and the sound of Dad opening and closing cabinet doors as he scavenges for tea.

"You sure you're ready for that, honey?" Mom says. "Because last time—"

"Let her try again," Digby says. "I'll take you Monday morning. I'll come back for you after practice. No big deal."

Then he's gone.

BC spins in a circle and perches at my feet. Mom dunks her tea bag.

"Okay, good night, you guys," I say. "Thanks for the stellar edition of Jones Family Drama Hour."

172

"Do you want to talk about what's going on with you . . . on an emotional level? We're all here," Mom says.

I want to melt into a puddle of water on the floor. I want to let go, not to have to clutch so tight, but I can't. I have to hold on to the last of the good of this day, to the possibility of another day as strange and unfamiliar, but exciting as the one I've just had. So I hold on to boys with eyes like oiled wood and tree parts and doors opening and closing, a new world on the other side of every one.

"I'm trying," I say.

"Chamomile," Dad says. "Best medicine." He rubs my back briefly. "We can reconvene in the morning when everyone is more rested."

"Can't wait," I say, and I'm only being a little sarcastic.

"Eden," Digby's voice is low as a lullaby, as I walk by his open bedroom door a few minutes later, "I miss you."

I HOLD THE BOX FROM MADAME IN MY LAP AS THOUGH IT IS A BITING, STINGING THING.

I slowly unwrap the paper.

When I was twelve, I didn't want to live at home anymore. I decided I was going to move in with Madame, that it would be the best strategy for my career. Plus, I liked her better than my own family. She wasn't married, she didn't have kids, she was once a star so she knew all the ins and outs of the business, the industry. I had been outside her house, and it seemed big enough to fit me. If it turned out not to be, I was fine sleeping on the couch until she could make other arrangements, get a new house or whatever. What I needed was someone I could have totally to myself, who would see me as a whole person instead of half. She was perfect and already loved me, so I didn't even have to win her over.

I showed up at her doorstep with a carry-on suitcase I stole out of my dad's closet, stuffed with nothing but leotards and ballet shoes. The necessities.

Funny what you discover when you get behind someone's front door. It's never what you think it will be.

Madame might not have been married, but she definitely had a partner. A woman named Benita, who was still in her work clothes when I got there, on a Monday night in spring. I had met Benita before. She was at every opening-night performance and occasionally showed up at the studio, but I'd thought she was a friend. I had never considered that Madame had anything going on outside of ballet. It didn't seem that a person like her would have room for it. I assumed she danced and taught and slept, occasionally ate some food. End of Madame's story.

I had imagined so many things. We would be dedicated to each other. We would work in the studio, the two of us, until she made a star of me. When I won competitions, scholarships, when accolades rained down upon us, she would get me flowers, she would give me standing ovations. From the stage, our eyes would meet as she clapped and sobbed. She would be everything to me, and I would fulfill a latent need in her to be a mother. Win-win.

But why ever didn't I want to go home? Benita and Madame asked me. Was I in an abusive situation? Did I fear for my safety? Were my parents neglecting me?

175

After a minute scrambling for something to say to them that would convince them to let me stay (because inside, I knew I had lost this battle before it started), I confessed that my house was clean and safe, my parents clean and safe, too. I had a brother. I was the most important thing in his life, even more so than the ball he carried tucked in at his side at all times. I was never alone unless I wanted to be. I had never gone hungry. No one had ever touched me in anger. I had never even done my own laundry.

I didn't tell them, but I was fleeing because I was bored. I wanted to be my own person, the center of everything. Faced with two sets of perplexed brown eyes and a bowl of passion-fruit sorbet, I decided that, basically, I was evil and selfish.

Benita and Madame listened to me for hours, offered me a bowl of cherries when the sorbet was long eaten and cleared away, along with some cold, hard advice. They told me to go home and love my family. *It's what makes you,* Benita said, *for better or for worse. And when you've got what you've got, take it. People who really love you aren't easy to come by.*

Madame called my mom, who picked me up and explained to me for the first and last time on the way home how much she had wanted children, yes, but more than that, a little girl. How she and Dad had tried and tried. First there had been a turkey baster, then some egg sifting, and finally *in vitro*. She had withstood painful shots. She had gotten fat. She had stayed in bed as directed, read books, done a lot of crying. And then she had been rewarded for her patience and effort when the doctor informed her she would have not only one baby, she would have two, and one of those babies would be a girl. A *girl*. She wanted me more than anything, so much it terrified her. So if I felt she favored Digby, well, she was overcompensating.

I see Mom again as she was on the bed when I was in the In Between, how her whole body grieved, and it is only now that I believe what she told me that night so many years ago.

In the box, Chacott pointe shoes. The ones I so coveted when Madame and I went into New York that awful day. More white than pink, making the legs look even longer. They are the daintiest, the most spectacular of pointe shoes. They are Cinderella's slippers. I'd suspected Madame might reward my accomplishments someday with a pair, the way she encouraged me to hold them, try them. She had her friend Nadja take all my measurements. But I didn't earn them then, and I haven't since.

Yet here they are, specialty made-to-order magic just for me, direct from Japan.

My hands shake as I put in my earbuds and hit Play on

Mozart. I haven't listened to classical music since before, and the violins immediately undo me. I reach into my side table where I keep a flashlight, a compass, several books, and a sewing kit.

I stuff the shoes' toes with lamb's wool, then darn with the ribbons and elastics that came in the box. With BC at my feet, I draw thread through the satin, and I think about feet, mine especially.

How they are a pearly, clean white now.

How there was that time a muscle actually burst through and I danced on it anyway because there was a performance and there was nothing else to be done. For years, I would come home nights, fill up a tub with ice, and force my feet into it until they were numb and stopped hurting. On days that didn't work, there were Epsom salts and Tiger Balm. Sometimes all three on rotation. My excellent ugly feet.

Black-and-white posters of Anna Pavlova and Mikhail Baryshnikov look on in disapproval. I ignore them and sew. I loop. Loop elastic into the heel, the thread around the pointe for reinforcement, test it on my foot. I've done this so many times, it's automatic, replacing each pair of my pointe shoes as the old ones dissolved from use, but these ones are special. They feel like happiness.

I stretch them over my feet and arch.

BC pants and yowls, rolls on his back.

"Let's dance, doggie of mine."

BC crouches and jumps, waiting for instructions.

I hike up my sweats to the knee. My thighs burn almost immediately as I begin running through the most basic warm-up, but I keep going.

Demi-pointe.

Relevé.

Demi-pointe.

Again.

Again.

Again, Eden.

THAT SUNDAY NIGHT, I HAD A DREAM ABOUT JASMINE.

I saw her from a distance and knew it was her, in my guts and all my fear, though her arms and legs were more muscular than in the hospital room, ropy, and she was generally thicker than she looks lying in her bed, strapped to machines. Not withered. Not shrouded in membrane. She wore a white tank and jean shorts, like In Between, and her arms and legs bled with vicious scrapes and cuts. The sky, though, was clear and blue, the dirt around her red as Mars. She was at the edge of a cliff, pacing, as though about to step off.

I ran to her, and the more I ran, the farther away she got. So I picked up speed, put all my strength into it, until the landscape beside me turned to a fiery blur.

Then the ground was gone, but I didn't fall. Jasmine loomed above me, floating too, her mouth moving with words I couldn't hear. She raised her arms to reveal wings thick with writhing black flowers and brambles come to life, buzzing like bees. Instead of eyes were two flowers being pollinated by butterflies with lazy, fluttering wings. She reached for me. Tears streamed across her face, and I tried, tried to hear.

AFTER THAT DREAM, SCHOOL IS, LIKE, WHAT AM I DOING HERE?

I have trouble waking up. Trouble choking down oatmeal. Trouble getting into the Beast for the silent trip to school. But even with my trouble, I get ready for school and go, because like the family said, I'm not right, and if I want the spotlight off of me, I need to prove I am capable of something, to let them feel that what happened to me at the river didn't destroy me. I'm still the person they love and miss.

I can do this.

Once I'm at school, even as I'm cruising down the hall, giving hugs to people I don't know all that well and having conversations with curious grownups, I see Jasmine with those butterflies in her eyeballs, flapping their wings, suckling on flower meat, and I am distracted. I can't stop thinking about her.

I need to text Joe, tell him that we should meet at the hospital, maybe try talking to Jasmine again. She wanted to tell me something in that dream. Maybe something important.

Problem is I can't text Joe because even though we spent an evening together that felt eons long, we never exchanged information because, as has been confirmed on many occasions, I'm a moron.

Joe's ghost follows me around all morning, so I only feel half here. His hand on my cheek, the memory of him stroking my throat, the back of my neck, the kiss, even the apology. How flustered he was. I have to lean on lockers to get control of my breathing in the hallway. I stay there for so long that Mrs. Klein asks me if I would like to lie down in her office.

I almost take her up on her offer. Lying down sounds great.

But no, because, there's English, and Mr. Liebowitz, and everyone reeks of sweat and minty toothpaste and whatever they're using to cover up the sweat. And after English, it's AP bio, which has always been my favorite class. And what are we discussing today, my little maladjusted poppets?

Butterflies.

You bet.

Did you know that caterpillars basically completely disintegrate while they're in the cocoon? They liquefy, all but these discs that literally unfold, turn inside-out and become the butterfly. It would be like if, explains Mr. Gelrip, we carried around the seeds of our grown-up selves, as if everything we would ever become was already there. I doodle flowers and bloody butter-flies on the piece of paper in front of me, watch the videos flash on the screen.

I collect my catch-up work. The teachers didn't get a chance to ruin my life the first day I tried to come back, but now we have to face facts, and the facts are that if I don't get myself together on a whole bunch of levels, I'm not going to graduate. I have until the end of the semester and then in the fall I'm supposed to be on my own, and I really, actually don't want to live in my parents' basement. I need to focus.

I should call Madame back. Maybe today after school.

I should do a lot of things.

I can probably catch up on the schoolwork, but the rest of life seems like too much.

At lunch I venture into the chaos of the cafeteria, where I find Digby at a table with Parker and Reggie, and where the noise of all the talking and the smell of yeasty rolls nauseate me briefly.

I need to make up with my brother, to feel like things can go back, that everyone can go back, but instead of the loud, lively table we usually occupy, I find a dank, uneasy, low-frequency vibration permeates the place. Parker makes full eye contact with me, then turns his entire chair away.

"What's up with this?" I say. "Parker?"

Reggie says, "He's still hurt about what you said to him at the club in Philly."

"Geez." I nudge Parker. "Someone's got their sensitive pants on."

"A bunch of hurt people in here." Reggie says, and nods his head to the table next to us. "And you know what they say. Hurt people hurt people."

"Great. Everyone's mad at me. Except Lucille. So far," I say, as my brother slinks deeper into his seat. "Where is she?"

Reggie clears his throat. "Girl," he says, "shut up."

He points.

Elaine, Digby's newly ex-girlfriend, is sitting stick-up-the-butt-straight at the table next to Digby's with Zoe and Marin, their hair all perfectly coiffed. I swear I had forgotten she ever existed. *Zip.* Expunged. Digby and Elaine's relationship has faded, and I barely recognize her.

"Hi, Elaine!" I say, so loudly everyone jumps.

"Hi, Eden." She's midbite of an apple, and finishes chewing. "I'm glad everything turned out okay with your accident," she says. "That must have been scary." She fingers a chicken patty. "I would have come to visit you and everything, but you know . . ." She gathers herself, eyeing Digby. "Anyway, I'm glad you're okay."

I pat her shoulder, since she doesn't really seem open to

185

hugging. My brother cheated on her with my best friend, so that's not really surprising.

"The alternative would have been a bummer," Digby pipes in. "I mean, if Eden had died."

Elaine stares at him, one eyebrow arched. "You're talking to me. Really?"

"I'm just saying if Eden hadn't come out of it . . . her coma . . . it would have been hard for all of us," he finishes, finally.

The painful flailing.

Reggie whistles low.

"Yeah, that' s true," Elaine says. "It would have been hard. But don't. Don't ever talk to me again, okay, Digby?" Elaine stands, along with her friends, who do a really good job of backup scowling. She turns to me, her back to Dig. "Sorry your brother feels like it's okay to use your accident to try to make it seem like he's not totally disgusting. I'll see you later, Eden."

"Yeah, Elaine, take care."

They swish away in unison, heels clack-clacking on the floor. "Wow," I say, when she and her girls are gone. "She is so not into you. And I forgive you for using my accident as a failed olive branch."

"Yeah," Reggie says. "That hurt to watch."

Digby rests his face in his hands. "I am trying so hard," he says, muffled. "She won't let it go. But then, like, why sit next to me? Torture?"

"Naturally," I say. "So where did you put Lucille?"

"She's in the art room. Painting, I guess. Smokey lets her work in there whenever she wants." He can't help himself. He's proud.

"She's in there by herself?"

"I mean, what do you want from me?" Digby says. "She's her own woman. I can't exactly hold the brush for her. She can do what she wants." He shoves a handful of limp fries into his mouth. "And if she wants to paint at lunchtime, I support her."

"What a man," I say.

"Attacking my manhood now? Girls are the problem here, okay?"

"How is it being back?" Reggie says, a hand on my arm, steering me away from my own mouth.

"Basically," I say, forcing my eyes away from Digby, "I remembered why I'm grumpy all the time. Also learned some disturbing butterfly facts. Nature is a bitch."

"Excellent," Reggie says. "It's the most you can hope for in this fine educational establishment. Success!"

Digby sips out of a water bottle, nods to the chair where Elaine was sitting. "I've said sorry to her, like, a hundred times."

"Yeah, well," I say, "hell hath no fury like a woman scorned and stuff."

Digby pulls a chair out for me.

"Park," I say, sitting down, "I'm sorry about what I said at the club, even though you need to get over it. I got a little wasted."

"People tell the truth when they're wasted," he says. "Don't make like that's not what you think of me."

"No way," I say. "Now that I'm seeing through sober eyes, it's clear that your hair is totally hot."

"Yeah?"

"Yeah, totally. And not only the hair on your head. Also the ones on your chin."

Reggie drops his head and shakes it.

Digby laughs.

Parker throws his chicken sandwich back on his tray and stands.

"Screw you, Eden," he says. "For real. I'm going to eat outside. I'd rather freeze my balls off than deal with you."

"And my work here is done," I say. "Wonder twin powers activate!"

Digby and I fist-bump. And like that, I know everything is going to be okay.

SHE'S THROWING POTS, NOT PAINTING.

The wheel whirs, and Lucille adds water, shapes the clay, adds water, shapes the clay. Watching her, I think how much she has changed over the last few months. As much as me. More, maybe. She's a butterfly, for sure. She was melted down to nothing but goo and then rose up better. Even the way she sits, it's like she's taken command of the chair. There used to be an apology in everything for her. Now she's molding things into other things, making something out of nothing, totally focused, muddy to her elbows. I don't know how she takes care of Wren, her parents doing who knows what. She takes care of my brother, too. Maybe I am jealous. Not of her, of him.

The pottery wheel sits at one edge of the enormous space. It smells like paints in here, and there are spatters everywhere, on the walls, the floor, the table. It's the only room in the entire school with light from huge windows. One of them is cracked open, probably to keep anyone from dying from exposure to fumes, and every once in a while, a breeze ruffles some papers and I'm hit with freshness, possibility. I shouldn't disturb Lucille. I should let her work her own things out, since she can and she hasn't seen me yet. But I miss her.

"Why aren't you with your lover?" My voice echoes.

The whirring stops.

"Eden," she says, head tilting. "There you are. And gross," she adds. "You know how I feel about that word."

"You're the one who's gross. My brother?"

She sniffs. The thing we swore would never happen between us is happening, our lives separating us into two people. She is taking shape, while I have come apart. The irony is that soon she'll really be part of my family. No blood sister oath necessary. She is going to pledge herself to my brother. I can see her in her dress already, see them gazing at each other the way they do. It's going to be beautiful.

She is not mine anymore.

All the resentment I've been feeling flickers into something new. I wish I could catch her up on my life, but it's too late. She's already too far away. I know better now than to believe in real endings. Things only change. They become something else. We adapt. And sometimes we grow wings.

"Are you hungry?" I say.

I scoot into one of the tables and pull out the lunch I made myself this morning, a turkey and Brie sandwich. There's also a shake and a banana.

"I'm going to attempt real food now, and I need you to witness in case I die," I say. "Also, let's share. You haven't eaten yet, right?"

"No," she admits. "I figured I'd go get something when everyone is out of the caf."

I break off half the sandwich for her. She washes her hands in the utility sink and sits on the floor.

"And by everyone, you mean Elaine? She's already stormed off with her minions, so you're in the clear," I say.

She lowers her eyes. "I feel like it's the right thing to do not to put Digby and me in her face." How mature. "I wouldn't want to see it if I were her. Actually," she says, "the idea of him with someone else, of having to see that, makes me totally sick. I still remember what it was like having to watch them together, even though it was so different."

"Ah, the life of a succubus."

She crumples a stray piece of paper and throws it at me.

"I hate it," she says. "It's like I can't make up my mind. I love Digby so much I can't be sorry we're together, and I'm simultaneously so ashamed of what we did I can't forget it."

"I'm sorry, Lu."

"I like working in here alone," she says. "So it's not all bad. I can think."

"I'm proud of you."

"Yeah?" she says. "Why?"

"I think you're kind of amazing. What you've done. What you're doing. You did something real. Not everyone does that."

"Are you making fun of me?" she says, picking some leftover clay from under her fingernails.

"I'm being earnest as hell," I say. "I swear."

"You can't blame me for asking. You did slam your head on that rock."

"That's right, I did. Stuff changes when you almost meet your maker."

"Well." She looks to be considering whether or not to delve any further into what that means. "Digby and I have been avoiding having all the suckish conversations, like about what's going to happen when school's over and how we're going to keep on being together and still have lives. And what I'm going to do with Wren. I mean," she says, "do I leave her here with my dad or take her with me, if I'm even going anywhere? I have to go if I'm going to be with Digby. Because there's no way he's staying here. Not even if he wanted to."

"He shouldn't."

None of us should. The only thing there is to do in this town is work in a restaurant or cut hair. Cater like my mom, build houses like my dad. We should all get out of here and see something different. Anyway, Digby knows what school he's going to. Penn State. It's a done deal. And me? What about me?

"I'm not going to college. Not yet, anyway. I need more time to figure it out." She sighs a sigh from so deep in her that it shakes the room. "Blink, and it's graduation. Maybe," she says, "there won't even be an us after that."

"Please don't be an idiot," I say. "Of course there's going to be a you."

"Anything can happen at any time, though."

"Yeah."

"Doesn't it make you feel ooky?"

I think about this.

"Also," she says, "my mom called."

"What the hell?" I flop down next to her, but she turns her head away, and I think she's trying not to cry. It's easier if we don't admit it.

I get it. Her mom's been gone all year. She wandered off one day and never came back. I thought she disappeared into a parallel dimension for a while. Nice lady, but Laura was always a flake, the kind of person who would leave a baby in the car in the summer, not because of evil, but because of floating above the ground instead of gravity having the same effect on her as the rest of us. She seemed like she was okay with being fragile, used it as an excuse to be a crappy mom, to take care of herself instead of thinking about her kids. I hated her for that. Still do.

Could be worse, I guess. Like I said, she's nice enough.

"There were a few messages from her when I finally got a new phone," Lucille says, "but it took me a while to call her back."

"I don't blame you."

"I mean, what if I tried and her new number was disconnected? What if she didn't mean what she said on the messages? I don't think I could take it again. And Wren . . ."

"How long ago did she call, Lu?"

She doesn't answer.

"Months?" I say.

"Months," she says, nodding. "A couple, anyway. She called a few weeks into your accident, and I just answered her this week."

"So? What does she want?"

"She wants to see us. Has some new boyfriend in California. Wants Wren to go move there with her. Says she's stable now. Wren doesn't know about any of it yet. Digby wants us to go visit her, maybe for spring break. Check out what's going on with her before we go sending Wren."

"So what?" I say. "You're moving to California with your mom?"

Lucille shrugs. "Only if everything falls apart with Dig, and it would only be to keep Wren safe. I don't know if I trust her to be a good mom anymore. I feel like sending Wrenny there would be leaving her on a raft in the middle of the ocean."

"So you'll keep Wren here until you guys decide what to do?"

"Yeah. Mom mentioned selling the house. I think she wants the money. If she does that, we can't live there anymore. So yes, there's a lot. It's a lot." No Lucille in that house seems impossible. She's part of that block. That block is part of her. But then, it was the same for me.

"Okay, so now it's your turn." She props herself up on one elbow.

I try to imagine what I might say about what's going on with me. It's not college, that's for sure. It isn't any of the things I thought it would be this year. In order to explain it, I would have to start over, tell her everything that happened from the accident to when I woke up, all the way until now. Her phone buzzes. She types, then turns her attention back.

"You were going to tell me things?" she says.

I really consider it for a moment.

"Only that I love you," I say.

"I love you too," she says.

We eat side by side, watching the clouds float outside the windows. She smells like oranges and the chalky, minerally scent of clay, and I want to tell her how her eyelashes are so long and badass, I can see them fluttering in my peripheral vision. I want to tell her that when I almost died, it was her I went to first in my dreams, in my thoughts. I went to our memories, our place. I don't say anything, though, because it's been such a long time since I sat with my best friend like this, in perfect silence.

I squeeze her a little tighter, move even closer, and feel her smile against my cheek.

From Almost Dead: True Stories of the Afterlife

What happened to me?

There's things that are better forgotten. Like car accidents where not every-one survives.

Two things I'll tell you, though:

One, there's nothing to be afraid of.

And two, lots more people here on earth are already dead than know it. You can have a body that works and not be living.

Put that in your pipe and smoke it. Now leave me alone.

— Mandy Groomer, 16, high school student

"CHOP WOOD, CARRY WATER."

"Come again?" I say.

Marlene Gat is in an excellent mood today, brimming with good advice. She waves her hand about in front of her.

"Have you ever heard that expression, Eden? It's from the Zen Buddhist religion."

"Like 'what is the sound of one hand clapping?'" I shake my head. "Never went in for that sort of thing."

"That one keeps you thinking. But this is more practical advice."

"I'm telling you that I'm confused about the nature of existence, and you're telling me to chop wood and carry water?"

She claps her hands. "Exactly," she crows. "Brilliant!"

"Okay," I say. "Calm yourself. You're going to herniate."

"Eden, please listen."

The woman loves the sound of her own voice above all other things.

"Go on." I tuck my hands under my chin and bat my eyelashes. "Please, I'm all ears."

"When things are complicated and you don't understand what's happening, simplifying and looking for ways to be in the present moment can help you to gain clarity."

Oh, for Pete's sake.

"When you wonder how the world works, do the dishes." She leans back like she's just given me the key to everything, a Cheshire Cat grin on.

"Seriously?" I say. "*That's* your great advice?"

"Well, yes," she says. "It is. Practice it. I promise it works. When you find yourself overwhelmed, do something simple that requires physical attention on your part."

"This is not what I thought therapy would be like." I pick a brown leaf off the plant on the table next to me.

"Me neither." She pours some tea. "You make me work for my paycheck, Eden."

I would take offense, but when she smiles at me, it goes all the way to her eyes.

THERE ARE SECRETS
IN THERE.

I can tell from the paint bubbling and peeling on the greenhouse's sides, all rusty. It's getting dark now. After therapy I rushed to the flower stand, which sat abandoned. So, I climbed up to Joe's apartment, where I had an awkward interaction with Norma, during which she told me she was going to be one of those people who is killed by the flu and I should stay away from her. She then directed me here.

I knock on the greenhouse door, and when there's no answer, I peer through one of the many windows. I can't see much.

"Norma?" Joe appears out the side door. "Why'd you knock—"

One glance at him, and it's nerves upon nerves eating nerves and spitting them out again, then consuming more nerves. "I just died inside," I say. "My heart literally stopped beating. You killed me."

It's not true. My heart is beating double-time, triple, a thousand times what's right. If I had not acknowledged his dead sexiness in my mind the other night, if I had pretended to myself that he is annoying and completely unattractive, if he had kept his mouth off of mine, I would not be having this problem.

Denial is super useful. That's the advice Marlene Gat should be giving: Pretend your life away. Stay safe. Face nothing.

Joe is in a work shirt and jeans, sweating in the winter cold, and holds a pot of something, maybe dirt, in one hand. The tool belt he has slung around his waist is compelling.

I try to concentrate, to feel my feet. "You gardening?" I say, idiotically.

He examines the pot in his hand. "Seaweed," he says. "It's feeding time for the plants."

I think momentarily that it's only three blocks to the bus, that I can walk/run there and never see Joe again. I can play this off in some way and save my pride, because he is so not happy to see me. And who shows up at a person's green-slash-hothouse uninvited, Eden?

And then he smiles and my knees are lava and I'm not going anywhere.

"Want to come in?" He puts a hand on the small of my back to guide me through the door, and when he takes it away again, I miss it.

Then I'm in a world of green and white, so warm my

long-sleeved shirt and jeans hang heavy, like I walked into a wet sponge. I have found the portal I was looking for, because this is a whole other world.

I run my fingers over the juicy leaves of a plant dripping with pollen.

"Watch that," he says. "Pollen is messy. Stains your clothes."

"You grew these?"

He nods. "Me and Norma and my dad."

"People have all kinds of talents," I say. "Weird things. Salinger said something like that."

"Who?"

"He wrote *Catcher in the Rye*." I watch him take scoops of the meal from a bucket and put one in each pot. "Salinger said something like maybe even bores are terrific whistlers. I think about that whenever someone seems lame. Like we all have a secret talent." I catch myself. "Not that you're lame. I didn't mean that. Neither is Norma. Or your dad."

Joe shakes his head a little.

"I can't whistle," he says. "Watch."

He can't whistle at all. He puffs his cheeks, licks his lips, blows. Nothing.

"You're faking," I say.

"Not."

"Well, you make things grow," I say. "You make things . . . bloom."

"It's just plants."

But as he clips and waters and does what he's doing, he doubles in size. When someone is doing the thing they're best at, they open.

"I kill all living things," I say. "Except my dog."

I've been wandering, but pause because whatever I'm looking at right now is magnificent.

"What's this?" I say.

Joe purples. "It's mine," he says. "An orchid topiary. It's just something I made. I grew it. Am growing it. I mean, it's not for sale."

It's literally the most perfect thing I've ever seen. An orchid umbrella.

"I won't steal it. Or try to buy it. Scout's honor."

"Thanks. Orchids don't like to be overwatered, but they do like it humid. That's why it's so intense over here."

"I could never do this," I say. "This is perfect."

"I bet you never really tried," he says, with the confidence of someone doing something that comes easy.

"Not true," I say. "I'm not allowed to touch my mom's flowers because she's smart."

"No one ever taught you right. That's all."

Or I didn't show any interest.

"You didn't tell me you have a dog," he says. "What's its name?"

"Beaver Cleaver. We call him BC. He's white and fluffy and extremely goofy."

"A dog person. Interesting."

"Oh, you thought you knew me already? No, sir. I'm a very surprising person."

"Oh, really?"

"Yes. Not only have I visited the other side, in my spare time, I squeeze the toothpaste from the middle. I like sandalwood soap, even though my mom sings terrible classic rock when she smells it. And I can't wait to eat pasta. I feel like I haven't eaten enough of it. I have a deficiency."

"Should I take notes?" he says. "Because I will, like, if there's going to be a test later."

There's going to be a later? Yes, please.

"I thought you would be at the hospital," I say. "Did you go see her today?"

"No." He fusses about with cans and mixtures. "I needed a break."

"But . . ."

"I needed a break, Freckles," he says. "Okay? Like, really. From both of you, actually. Had to think."

"Because you kissed me?"

"You kissed me back," he says. "A lot."

"A lot," I agree.

"It's not funny, Eden." To my amateur eye, it seems like he's pruning a little too vigorously. "I can already tell if we were together, it would drive me crazy how you make a joke out of everything."

"If we . . . Don't you think you're, like, jumping the gun?"

"Am I?" he says. "Something about you. Fuck!"

He drops the seaweed, and it goes flying everywhere in big smelly clumps.

"Something about you tells me not to play," he says. "I don't think this is a game. Do you?"

I don't know what to say. I wish he would kiss me again, run his hand across my belly, repaint me lovely with his eyes.

"I'm sorry I'm messing with your inner peace," I say, trying to find a dustpan and broom, trying not to jump on him. I hesitate, hand them to him. "Not to add to the disruption, but I think we should go back to Gigi's."

He sweeps the floor without looking up.

"So you came for Jasmine?" He sounds mad.

"Yes," I say. Then I think about the way I dashed past her room when I was looking for Joe. Didn't even say hi to the nurses and certainly didn't give Jasmine a sponge bath or rub her feet or anything. Just scurried on by. OMG, I'm using a fellow coma girl for nefarious, selfish reasons. Because I really like this boy. I like a boy! "No," I say.

Joe tosses the meal back into the bucket, then takes off his gardening belt and lays that down, too. His sweat, when he gets close, smells like cookies, I swear, hand to my heart. I did not, could not, have made that up.

"I did come here," I say, "because of her. But also," I kick my backpack full of gym clothes, on the floor at my feet, "I put on real clothes for you after physical therapy so you could see me in something other than sweats. It's so upsetting, Joe, but I think I like you. Really."

"I like your Beatles shirt," he says.

He hands me a single white rose.

"And you," he says. "I like you too." He leans against the counter and smirks at me in a way that sinks my battleship, but then he turns dark. "But I can't. There's something wrong with the whole thing. You appearing when Jasmine wouldn't, when I wished she would. You waking up. You and Jaz. Without Jaz, there wouldn't be this." He shakes his head. "I don't know. It doesn't seem right."

"The shirt was my grandma's," I say, when I can't tolerate the staring contest we're having anymore, can't stand how awesome I think it is that he cares about right and wrong.

"You like me?" he says, finger in the hollow of my throat again, tracing my collarbones.

"I mean, I think you're . . ." I say. "You want to hold my hand and walk around the playground?"

"Eden," he says, "please shut up."

I think he's strong. His arms, his chest, it's all decidedly decided. But not only that. His mom. His life. Everything that's happened to him. It's like he knows himself, but he doesn't know what to do with me. He puts one hand on either side of my waist, on the wood behind me, and I do shut up. For a second.

"I thought you didn't have time for flirting."

He grazes my lips in response.

"If you kiss me again, you can't apologize."

He does. I totally attack him. I kiss him, my arms around his neck. I'm a selfish person, and this is weird on some level, and I take full responsibility for this warm, melty, salty, soft-lipped yumminess.

Wait.

It's perfect.

It's not my lips, it's my everything.

207

Oh.

#$&@)())#)***^

I think my brain is shorting out.

%^@(*^

. . .

But.

. . .

. . .

My mind was blank for a second. For several seconds. I mean, there was nothing. No thoughts. It was so good. It was a miracle. More kissing. More of that.

. . .

. . .

. . .

I open my eyes to look at Joe and maybe report to him how glorious he is, but instead I pull away and drop my mouth open. I try to scream, but no sound comes out. As I look over Joe's shoulder, every white flower in the greenhouse is being sloshed over with black, transforming in front of me, turning light to dark as though someone is pouring oil over each one. Joe's topiary. No!

"Hey," he says. "Easy, Freckles. You're nailing me with that rose."

Droplets of blood pepper his arm from the thorns.

"I'm sorry." I look at my hand. "I didn't mean to hurt you."
The rose he gave me is the last thing in this room that remains white. The only thing.

"Hey, are you okay?" he says, searching. "No, you're not okay. Come on." He ushers me to the door. "Trust me. I got you."

JOE GUIDES ME ACROSS THE STREET TO GIGI'S.

She doesn't seem surprised to see us, but she isn't jumping for joy or anything. She lets us in, takes one look at me, and starts mumbling to herself in French. She settles me at the table, and Joe falls into the chair next to mine.

"I'm sorry." He leans in to whisper to me. "I . . . Was it the kiss? Did I . . ."

"Yes, Joe." My teeth are still chattering. "The taste of your luscious lips broke me and caused temporary psychosis."

He sits back in the chair, never taking his eyes off me.

"They told me you would be coming back," Gigi shuffles her deck of cards. "I was prepared."

"They?" Joe says.

"The spirits." She indicates the air around us. I can't help but glance, in case there's an orb hovering around my head.

"Aw, man. What the hell is going on?" Joe lays his head on the table and bangs it a couple times.

Good to know we're all crazy here.

"Medicine," Gigi says, presenting me with a cup. I sniff it, relieved to find it isn't eye of newt or anything. Just plain, hot coffee.

I take a sip and immediately begin to feel normal again. I have to not think about flowers bleeding black onto everything, and I'll be A-OK.

Gigi lays out cards into a cross formation on the table, boomeranging back and forth between them, tapping a finger down every once in a while. "*Bon.*" She folds her hands in, still watching the cards. "I think whatever you are seeing has to do with Jasmine, with what we discovered yesterday. In my opinion, if you want to understand what is happening to you, you must try to go back, to get to the bottom of it."

Back. How do you get back to somewhere that exists only in your mind?

"Gigi." I'm thinking of just before I had my accident, and all the questions I had running through my head. "If there really are spirits and all that, why don't they tell us what's going on? Why is everything such a mystery?"

Gigi wipes hands on her apron. "Don't you find puzzles fun?"

"I'm not a crossword person," I say. "And sudoku makes me angry."

"Well, I think the spirits delight in puzzles. They love leaving clues and riddles and watching us all try to sort it out."

"So life is some kind of scavenger hunt?"

"More or less," she says, petting one of her pewter owls like it's alive.

"Pretty high stakes," Joe says.

"What is the worst that can happen, eh?" she says. "You die! So what?" She throws up her arms. "We all die."

She stacks her cards and wraps them in a red cloth, then pulls stuff out of her apron. A few rocks of different colors, a shell. I drink slowly, let the warmth of the coffee soothe me, letting Joe being next to me soothe me, too.

"We'll need to hold hands," Gigi says.

"Is this going to be a séance?" I whisper to Joe.

"A séance is for the dead," Gigi says. "This is about connecting the three of us to each other and then attempting to go another step and connect to Jasmine. The spirits say to try." She takes the cup from me and places it in the sink. I don't ask her why the spirits can't do us a solid and handle this themselves. From a drawer under her sofa, Gigi retrieves a blue cotton tablecloth with a circle embroidered on it, separated into eight sections of different colored thread and spreads it over the table. In the middle, she places a white candle and lights something bundled up and green.

212

"Sage," she says, and blows the smoke toward me.

"The other day you said I was still there," I say. "With Jasmine. What did you mean? Where?"

She pauses and watches me, assessing. "There is part of you that has not come all the way back. Mostly, but not all. And for Jasmine, she cannot yet get free. May I?"

It takes me a second to realize she's pointing at the white rose on my lap.

"I only need a few petals." She puts them into a clear glass of water. "We must have all the elements." She takes a white porcelain owl from her shelf. "And a little help from my spirit animal. You'll do fine, *cher*," she coos as she puts it next to the candle. Then she turns down the light. "Okay," Gigi says. "Close your eyes."

I don't want to.

"Give me your hands. Now close them. Go on." She's so close her breath tickles my ear. "It will be okay, *chérie.*"

One hand goes to Joe and the other to Gigi, one palm wet, the other hot and dry. I wait for Gigi to give instructions, but she doesn't. There's nothing. Silence. After a few minutes I can hardly feel them. I see some colors, a silver, some gold, a light blue. But that's a normal thing to see when you have your eyes closed for a long time and there's a candle flickering in front of you.

Right?

She's here.

Jasmine.

And I see her, eyes bright and clear, no blood anywhere. She kisses me on my cheek, and I hug her, and the darkness and sadness that have been on me so tight are lifted. I am free, and I want to run far away from everything that's happening back there in that other place with all the hard things, all the pain. She grabs hold of me and then we do run together. But we don't run off a cliff. We run into a meadow. It's blooming, blooming black flowers that are not frightening, not here. They're alive and huge, almost as tall as me, soft like velvet, like a baby's cheek, like Joe's heart.

Joe.

I remember.

I need to go back to Joe.

I need Jasmine to come with me.

I tug on her. We're in an ocean, wave upon wave of blossoms. I see no way out. It's the same in every direction.

You can tell me what these are, I say to her, not letting go of her hand. I won't. She has to come with me. *Tell me. What do the flowers mean?*

Her mouth opens.

214

She's underwater. We both are. The meadow is underwater. Like before. Beforebeforebeforebefore.

Jasmine touches my cheek. Bubbles come from her mouth.

I'm sorry, I think. *I can't hear you.*

She pushes me.

I don't want to go. Come with me. Come back to Joe.

Already I feel the lull, the softness and sweetness of this place. The home of it. If I don't leave now, I never will.

Her face turns in on itself, and she shoves me.

I zoom backwards through infinity. I'm nauseated and dizzy.

"Eden!" Gigi is in my face, closer than Jasmine was, and I scramble back until I'm small in my chair. "You come back!"

I can't. I don't want to.

"You can! See?" she says to Joe. "How easy it was for her to get there?" She snaps her fingers. "Like that."

I failed. I didn't get Jasmine to come back. She wouldn't. She didn't want to. I have to try again. More. Harder.

"Did you . . ." Joe asks, hand on my back. "Did you find her?" He is so hopeful, his face wide open.

It's not me he wants. It's her.

I move faster than I ever have. Joe behind me. His hand on my wrist. I'm out the door, walking now as quickly as I can in

215

the freezing, biting cold. I know Joe is saying things to me, ask-ing me questions. I know it's not fair to ignore him.

But I can't stop, can't talk because if I do, the last of Jasmine will disappear.

I'M CHARGING JASMINE'S ROOM WHEN SPOCK BLOCKS MY PATH.

Part of me recognizes that storming a hospital room isn't super balanced, but I want to touch her, to hold her. I want to be somewhere she can find me so I can hear what she's trying to tell me. Spock glances back and forth from Joe to me, and folds his arms across his chest.

"Miss Jones," he says.

I'm still not quite right. Everything is so blurry I can't see what's in front of me. Only Jasmine. Jasmine and the flowers.

"You're looking out of breath," Spock says. "Would you like to come sit down?"

I eye Jasmine. She's in the bed. She's not yelling or screaming. She hasn't woken up. She's simply there. Limp. Tubes doing their slithering thing.

Spock directs me away from Jasmine's room and points at a chair.

I shake my head.

"Let me guess," he says. "You'd rather stand."

But not for the reasons he thinks. Because I can't sit. I can't sit right now.

"That's it," Spock says. "Let's try breathing. In through the nose, out through the mouth. Good. Good."

"I saw her." All at once there's hysteria. I want to laugh, but as soon as I do, I will cry. "I saw Jasmine like she was right here, not a dream. Real. And she was trying to talk to me."

"Don't worry about her right now," he says. "You need to get control. Focus on me."

I can't. Ican'tcan'tcan't.

"No, don't look at him. Look at me." It's Joe. He followed me. "I'm right here," Joe says.

I do look at Joe. Stare right into his eyes. He holds my wrist and inhales. And I do it with him, fill my lungs with clean air. And after a minute, there's nothing but us.

"I saw her," I say to Joe as soon as I am capable, barely aware that Spock is here too, that he is listening. "For real, Joe. I saw her like you, standing in front of me. She touched me. She kissed my cheek."

Joe's hand goes there, where she kissed me. "Eden," he says.

"Listen to me." I hold him by the wrist, make him look at me, and not with that look like he feels sorry for me. "I'm telling you, Joe. Jasmine. I saw her behind my eyes. Really. And you can think I'm crazy, and I don't care. I don't know what she said, but she's there." I turn to Spock. "So don't pull tubes or disconnect anything, okay?"

Spock freezes.

"Don't tell me it isn't real, and don't kill her," I say, looking at both of them. "She's still here."

I sit, or collapse. I need to sleep, to rest. I know it. My body has had enough.

"I'll be right back, Miss Jones," Spock says.

Rita glides down the hall. "What are you doing out here, baby? Are you all right?" She hands me a cup of ice chips, wipes at my brow.

"I'm okay," I say, pushing her away.

"You come to see Miss Jaz?"

"Yes." I look back to the bed, to the tubes, to the motionless almost dead Jasmine, as Rita goes on down the hall, to the next person, the next nearly dead.

Joe and I take our positions in the chairs by her bed, Jasmine's hand in mine. I wait for her to cling to it, to show signs of life. Still nothing. She could wake up right now. So why won't she?

"You let go of us," Joe says in a low voice. He double-checks over his shoulder to make sure we're alone. "We were sitting at the table, and almost right away, you dropped our hands. We tried to talk to you, but your eyes rolled back in your head and you shook. Like a seizure. We couldn't wake you up. I shouldn't have taken you over there. I didn't know what else to do." He leans forward, elbows on his knees.

"Jasmine wanted to say whatever she wanted to say really badly. So don't, okay?" I make Joe meet my eyes. "Don't disconnect her or whatever."

"Okay," Joe says. He's quiet for a minute. "Do you think this means . . ."

"She'll come back?" I ask. I don't know. And I don't know what to hope for, either. If Jasmine comes back, I lose Joe. If she doesn't, I lose Joe. Where does that leave me? I don't want to be without Joe, especially now, as his hair tickles the back of my hand, sending shock waves all through me. I think I love him. I think I might. This is a disaster.

Spock is back. "Jasmine's had a rough day," he says, makes some notes on her chart. "I'm afraid her brain function is diminishing rapidly," he says to Joe. "Sometimes there's a sudden decline, and we can't really explain it."

"I think I'm going to go home," I say, standing. I need to get away from here, to think, to be away from Joe.

"Let's go," Joe says.

"No. You stay here," I say. "You should stay with her. I'm crazy," I say. "I've totally lost my mind, and I need to think. I can take the bus. You . . . do this." I indicate Jasmine, the room, his life.

"Miss Jones," Spock says, when I'm almost to the door, "you wanted to know what happened when I was in my coma, what I saw?"

"Sure," I say, though I'm not sure at all.

He looks at his watch, takes a breath, glances at Joe. "I saw my family, all around me. Then I think I wandered a little. Ah, God," he says, "it was so nice. Best memories I've ever had, and I was almost dead. So relaxing. So free. But I came back, and when I did, I knew I was going to spend my life well. That was the tradeoff for me."

"What?" I say.

"I get to know how good it will be when I die, and still stay put here on earth. I don't get the luxury of the questions about what happens."

He seems to be waiting for me to say something, but I don't, and after a minute, he looks at his watch, makes an excuse, and leaves quietly, feet hardly touching the ground.

I put my arms around Joe as soon as Spock is gone. I feel like I might never again. Like this might be the end for us. "Bye for now," I say to Joe.

221

Joe looks from me to Jasmine and back again. "Nope," he says. "Weren't we going to bowl?"

"That was forever ago," I say, even though it was only a few days ago.

"So what?" he says. "Come on. Let's go do that. Let's bowl. Oh, yeah." He mimes a strike. "I can bowl my ass off."

"Now?" I say.

"Yeah, why not?" He puts his hand on my waist. "It's been a hard day. Let's play, Freckles."

WE'RE IN THE
BOWLING ALLEY.

There's a thrash-metal mosh pit that starts somewhere behind my sternum. The band is in my throat. There are three lead guitarists, and none of them really know how to play their instruments. The drummer is in my temples, and the wallflowers sway in my fingertips.

I glance at Joe, and everything gets violent again, loud.

I wish it would not be strange if I pulled out my notebook and paper, because I need to. I have things to say. Lists are so much better when you can look at them. In fact, you could learn pretty much everything you need to know about someone by looking at the lists that person makes. Grocery, to-do, and if you're like me, you can turn anything into a list. If you take a problem down to bullet points, the whole thing feels more manageable.

Possible triggers for internal maelstrom:

• Exhaustion masked as exhilaration

223

- Some sort of mental breakdown due to stress
- Brushing up against the occult
- Hunger
- Joy (?)

I haven't been bowling since Lucille's tenth birthday party. Fact: That party was horrible. Fact: I never did better than a gutter ball without assistance. The bowling alley put up the lane guards without asking, which ruined it for everyone else and also me. That party was in this very bowling alley. Fact: This is the site of my greatest humiliation. Why did I suggest it?

I'm wishing Lucille was here right now, because I don't know what the hell I'm doing, and she's a frighteningly proficient bowler. Her dad was on a league when we were little. I remember him leaving the house with the brown leather bag that held his bowling ball, cigarette dangling from his mouth, keys jingling in his free hand. He taught her everything about the sport, which has remained as mysterious to me as Jupiter. Whatever. They know nothing about a fouetté, so eat that, bowling experts.

This time of night there aren't any little kids, no birthday candles being blown out, nothing to kick my violent bowling memories into high gear. It's pitchers of beer all around us, and a lot of yelling, plus pinball machines, pool tables, and air hockey. It's loud and bright and smells like fry grease and sweaty shoes.

"You know what?" he says, after we get our bowling shoes on and check out the lane we've been assigned. "Is this a totally off thing to be doing right now?"

A red-faced blond lady in a bright purple T-shirt high fives her kids and shakes her arms in victory.

"What else is there?" I say. "When life gives you surrealist nightmares, you bowl."

And that's when he kisses me, and I turn to face the sun, and bloom.

WHEN I GET HOME, I DECIDE TO CLEAN OUT THE GARAGE WITH MY DAD.

Mom is catering a party, as the note on the counter told me, and will be back late. Digby is at Lucille's, I'm sure. And Dad is here, doing what he does when he needs to sort something out. My mother doesn't suffer clutter, and the garage is the only place exempt from her reign. So sometimes, when he needs somewhere to go besides his office, he comes here and puts things in new places. Or, we don't know what he does, really.

"You're going to help?" he says, when I appear in jeans and a T-shirt, hair up, and get an industrial bristle broom from the wall.

"I mean," I say, "you don't have to look *that* shocked."

"Why?" he says, totally flummoxed.

I would like very much to get all indignant about his confused facial expression, but it's true, I've never voluntarily done anything related to domesticity.

"Therapy," I say, and he nods, accepting my answer without further question.

This is what I love most about Dad. He once told me the world is capricious as a baby, so he rolls with the punches and aims for survival.

Anyway, I'm not totally lying about my reasons for being out here. It does have something to do with Marlene Gat and her *chop wood, carry water* theories. Something to do with thinking things have gotten so complicated and bizarre that cleaning out the garage is the right thing to do after bowling, after insane ghosts, and more, more kissing and cautiously braver hands.

We did so much kissing my lips are bruised beneath the surface. There's no discoloration, but every time I smile or talk, it's all Joe.

I sweep and move boxes to get behind them. Dad's organizing tools on a shelf, but he stops and watches me, leaning on a rake.

"You're moving again," he says. "Almost like you used to."

I take all the glass jars off a shelf and dust underneath.

"It seemed so hard I was afraid you were never going to be easy walking again. But look at you now. And you're so different than when you first woke up."

"Not a bitch, you mean?"

He reddens. "Moodiness is part of the recovery."

"I might have taken it a little far, though, right?"

"Maybe," he says. "But I think we got off easy. They said it could take months, and here you are. I'm proud of you," he says. "Even if I have no idea what you're doing in the world these days."

The lines on his face, the hair. My dad.

"I promise I'll tell you everything soon. But for now, can we not talk, Dad?" I say. "I really need to hang out with you and not talk."

"Yeah, honey," he says. "Sure."

It smells a little like oil and dust in here. There are no comatose people, nothing is coming after me. I can think about this day, about what it is to feel like someone is with you even when they're not, like traces of them have imprinted on you, so they're a flavor, a wisp, *the beautiful half of a golden hurt* (Gwendolyn Brooks). I didn't realize how much is frightening and exciting and possible, how much is in a choice.

BACK ON THE CLIFF.

Back in the dream.

Joe and I teeter at the edge of the cliff where Jasmine was a few nights ago.

He throws stones into the ravine, one by one, pebbles at first, then rocks so big he can hardly lift them. Still he struggles. Still he manages to get them off the ground and cast them down. I sit on a bench so cold on my skin it burns like I am a slowly disintegrating block of dry ice, and I wait for the sound of the rocks hitting the ground.

It never comes.

His spine ripples under his T-shirt like a cobra as he launches.

Toss.

Toss.

Toss.

"Joe." I want him to stop, to talk to me.

When he lurches toward me, black flowers pierce his arms, and he falls to the ground.

DR. MARLENE GAT
IS EXTREMELY SMUG.

"I'm so glad this is going well," she says, flipping through my journal. "This is simply wonderful." She slaps it shut and keeps it on her lap. I want to take it away. "Eden, this is really great. I don't mean to overstate things. I know you have a lot going on and things you'd like to improve, make progress with. But this is a step, a big one. So many fantastic things in here. Greenhouses, flowers . . . I love those, too!" She indicates her office. "I want to thank you for sharing with me. You could have kept it to yourself or even not told me you'd written in it at all, but you didn't. You were open and brave. And I am really honored to have earned your trust."

I trust you not, Marlene Gat.

Not with specters or black flowers, not with first kisses, or second and third ones, or with witches and coma girls like me. Not with secret lists and crazy dreams and a desperate discomfort. Not even with family scuffles and changing besties and dance shoes. But it does make a person dizzy what can happen

230

in a week. That's one thing a weekly therapy session is good for. To remind you what has happened, that you are no longer the same person you were seven days ago. That in seven days, everything has changed.

"I've been eating," I say. "Real food."

"And?"

"It's so good. Everything is the best thing I've ever eaten. I have to go slow, but that's okay."

"Slow is good," she says. "Better. Longer lasting."

I think of Joe.

"So," she says, from back in her seat, where she is still beaming and giving me an I-have-conquered-your-adolescent-psyche look. "Now let's talk next steps. Perhaps we can discuss college applications? I see you have them down here as something you love. Have you made progress in that department?"

I have moved the stack of applications from the right to the left of my desk. Does that count?

"Some," I say.

"Well, do you know where you would like to go? There's still time. And of course you could write a fantastic essay, about your accident, your post-accident aspirations."

"I don't know what I want to do anymore. I wanted to go to New York. I was going to audition for summer programs and see what happened from there."

"Why don't you tell me about that?"

"About what? I don't have anything to say. My dance future is over. The show has been canceled."

"Why is that?"

"Because of my accident. Because my legs don't work anymore."

"Have you tried?"

"Aren't you supposed to be aware of my limitations?" I prickle.

"I've been over your paperwork." She shuffles through her notes. "I see no reason you can't dance again." She looks up at me. "Am I missing something?"

"I don't know. I don't get to read that file. That's what they told me. That physical damage was going to make ballet impossible."

She looks at me for a long time, choosing her words.

"Eden," she says, "I know you have some recovery time ahead of you, some obstacles to overcome, but there's nothing in your paperwork that says you can't get back to it, and soon. Your mind, in its recovery process, may be trying to protect itself, might have generated that prognosis defensively."

"Are you saying I made it up?"

"I'm saying your brain might be trying to keep you safe."

It's silent for a long time.

232

"How do you feel about free will?" I ask.

She sits back. "Eden, do you know what deflection is?"

"Yes, because as you mentioned, I'm not stupid."

"Okay, then you know what you're doing."

"No, because listen."

She makes an acquiescent but tired hand gesture.

"Do you think we have destinies or fates?" I say.

"I don't know, Eden," she says. "It's enough work being a person, don't you think?"

"I always figured life is free falling, that there is no order to anything except maybe nature. You know, science."

"I'm listening," she says.

"Now I think maybe there's something going on, that maybe there are signs."

"Such as?"

I think of the flowers and what Jasmine was trying to tell me. What was it? "What if there are messages that point us where we need to go?" I say. "But what if something happens and we can't hear the messages that tell us about our destiny?"

"I'm so sorry, Eden, I'm afraid I don't follow."

"What if we have destinies and we miss the signs because we aren't paying attention? What if we miss out on our whole lives because of it?"

"If we have destinies, how can we miss them?"

233

"I don't know," I say, "maybe there's a difference between fate and destiny. It was my fate to fall. But now what? Where do I go? What am I supposed to do? I feel like something is pushing me, but I don't know what it wants."

Marlene looks bewildered and intense, leans forward, then writes something down on her pad.

"You're saying I'm crazy, right?" I say. "That's what you're writing in your notes?"

She sits up.

"Not at all," she says. "But we could all distract ourselves with philosophical questions, Eden. These are good things to think about, I suppose, questions about faith and higher powers. These are obviously things human beings wrestle with and can take a lifetime to truly come to terms with. But how do they help you now, with what you face, the choices you have ahead of you? As you like to point out, we only have a few more sessions left, and I would like to make good use of them."

"Okay, then," I say. "Tell me what to do. Because I'm trying to figure it out, and it's nuts out there."

"Rediscover yourself." She hands me my red journal. "Go find out what you like, what you want from your life in a concrete way. Circumstances are largely out of your control. You want to know what I think?"

Less and less every minute.

"Your accident proved to you that you aren't in control, and now you're afraid to try anything. You want someone to do it for you, to believe in something that takes the responsibility out of your hands. But don't do that. You're too special to do that. So don't worry about those big questions right now. Take steps. Real steps."

"Chop wood, carry water," I say. "Yeah, I know."

She sits back. "You can't change what life throws your way, free will or not. So you decide, Eden, how you're going to handle your life. Do you want to make a heaven of it, or a hell?"

I'M GOING TO TRY FOR HEAVEN, I GUESS, EVEN THOUGH IT FEELS LIKE HELL.

After therapy, during which I finally told Marlene about what happened during my coma and everything I saw and, surprisingly, she didn't have me put away, I went to spend a minute with Joe while he visited Jasmine.

I held her hand and he held mine, looking at me sideways.

And then, though I wanted to stay with him, to show him that the equation of us is a simple, a fixable thing, I came here to the Cherryville Community Auditorium, where I have danced a hundred dances. My parents sit on the board of the Cherryville Arts Commission, so they come to every show on opening night. They give their extra tickets to our friends. It's tradition and has meant even my brokest people can see me perform.

I wonder who I would have been in *Peter Pan*. Peter, probably. Then I would have flown. I'm on this lobby wall in black-and-whites from *Giselle, Swan Lake,* and of course *The Nutcracker*. I keep wanting to tell people, "That's me! Me!"

And now I'm going to be Girl in Audience instead.

Oh, how far we fall.

I'm kind of wishing I had discussed this with Marlene, but we ran out of time. I can imagine her pretty well. She would have told me to write about it in my journal, given me some good old platitudes, stuff about how to turn the morass that is my life into an exercise in enchantment and vivacity. *There's an opportunity in every moment, Eden!* That's what she would have said. Probably.

I've dressed for the occasion. My combat boots are shined up, and I put some makeup on, too, a fedora, and a red scarf around the throat. I'm currently looking at one of the pictures of me, trying not to get depressed.

"What's up, Red?" Reggie is here. "Careful you don't fall into your own picture and drown."

"I've never really checked these out," I say. "I was so bendy."

"Well," he says, "you look great in a tutu." He scans me up and down. "And this. I like it."

"Hides my scuffs, right?" I shift my scarf around.

He straightens his black shirt. His shoes are shined too.

"Looking dapper yourself," I say.

"Ah!" Mom approaches, arms out for a big hug, which she gives to Reggie and me simultaneously. "Isn't this wonderful? It must be a dream come true to get to relax in the audience,

Eden." She touches the brim of my hat. "No obligations, no stress, right? And you're looking wonderful."

Occasionally, my mom is stupendously full of it. My thought is that she does this when she's nervous, turns into a big faker. For instance, now, when she can't predict how I'm going to handle something.

"And did Lucille tell you her father is coming tonight?" Mom says.

"You tell me nothing," I say to Digby who's come up behind her. Although I guess I haven't been around much to hang out with. Not like we do what we used to, the two of us talking.

"Yes," Mom says, looking in her purse, then wiping at her nose with a handkerchief. "This is going to be wonderful. Can't wait to talk to Lucille's dad and hear all about his adventures."

"Adventures in the nuthouse?" I say. "Adventures in child abandonment? Adventures in alcoholism! No, I know! Adventures in adult aimlessness."

"Jesus, Eden," Digby says.

"The truth shall set you free," I say. "I don't judge, but come on."

Dad arches his eyebrows. Someone taps him on the shoulder, and he shakes a hand.

The auditorium is overly bright as they let us in so we can

238

find our seats. Nancy Clemens hands out programs and makes meaningful eye contact with me as she gives me one, letting me know she's aware of how hard this must be for me.

"Ugh," I say, too loudly.

"Lucille will be here soon," Digby says, like I'm worried, like that's all I have on my mind.

It's not.

What is on my mind is that it's wrong, me being in the audience. Not in every auditorium, only in this one. This one is mine. I prefer the greenroom, the busted-up couches, the never-filled vending machine, the pea-soup carpeting we all make jokes about. Everyone knows it was put down in the sixties when the auditorium was first built. Let's think for a second what kind of booming petri dish it's become. All the actors, the dancers. Some tomfoolery must have gone down on that carpet over the last fifty years. It's bacterial, but it's ours and we love it.

I know exactly what's happening backstage. Everyone will be gathering. They'll hold hands and squeeze each other's palms to pass the pulse around the circle until they are one continuous person. Then Madame will say something about how just because we're a small town doesn't mean our art doesn't have value and we're going to show the sons of bitches what we're capable of. Then she'll tell everyone to have a great show and leave to greet the audience.

Like I've summoned it by thinking of her, a familiar smell settles over me. *Eau de Dictatrice.* Madame leans down next to my seat.

"Hello, sweet Eden." She kisses me on the cheek. She has on dramatic eyeliner and bright red lips. "Thank you for coming. I officially forgive you for pretending to have a coma so you didn't have to hang from the rafters."

Mom laughs much louder than necessary.

"I wouldn't blame her," Madame says to Mom. "We all get fatigued, even when it comes to our passions."

She clacks her nails together like a praying mantis. "Have you opened my gift, Eden?"

"Yes." My eyes are immediately, viciously overfilled. What an awful person I've been. Not calling. Not saying thank you. Not saying anything. "Thank you."

"Stop," she says, standing. "Come now. No tears."

She's going to the back where she always stands during performances. I grab on to her hand.

"Eden?" she says.

"I want to come back." I pull her into a corner by the wall. People pass us and look. I don't care.

"But—" she says.

240

"No, please," I say. "I've been practicing alone. I've been try- ing. I want to. Will you help me?"

She pulls her cardigan around her waist and waits. The pause is eternal.

"I'm sorry," I say. "I know I was terrible at the Bolshoi, I know I failed you, and now I'm —"

"*Psht*," she says, waving me away. "You did nothing. They were doing complex, obscure routines. It was asinine, really. You would not have known those steps unless I had taught you." She lifts my chin. "I did not. That makes your experience that day my responsibility as your teacher. It has no reflection on you or your talent and capacity." She meets my eyes. "Or your future. You are an absolutely astonishing dancer," she says. "And I will help you in any way I can."

The sound of the audience has risen to a subtle din and in- side me, there is also a din. I'm alive, and Madame still believes in me. Inside: celebration, clapping, standing ovation.

I. AM. ALIVE.

Madame glances at her thin gold watch and then at the stage. "I'm sorry," she says. "I have to go. And now you will have the unfortunate experience of witnessing what happens to *Peter Pan* without you."

I nod.

"And, Eden," she says. "I will see you at five forty-five on

Monday morning. We will work weekdays for the remainder of the year until you graduate. I will not accept tardiness or laziness. We will get you back into shape, never fear."

I nod again. That means working hard before school and then physical therapy after school. Long days, and that's not even taking into consideration college, what I'm going to do about that, about catching up on my work so I can graduate.

Chop wood. Carry water. One thing at a time.

"You've got some mascara," Mom says when I sit back down. She spit shines my eyes.

"You all right?" Reggie asks from two seats away.

I nod.

"Oh, hi!" Mom says, her voice sliding up an octave, as Digby, Lucille, Wren, and their dad shimmy in to the row. "Eden! Say hi to Tony!"

I wave. Lucille's dad, Tony, is scruffy, cute, and wearing a brown cord jacket over an old T-shirt. You would never know anything momentous was happening, that this is his first time out with his daughters since his nervous breakdown, except that he looks like he spent a long time on his hair. It's greasy and combed down.

"So glad they let you out tonight," Mom continues.

"You did not just say that," I whisper to her.

242

"Lovely to see you!" she finishes, looking about self-consciously.

"You too," Tony says. "Nice to see everyone. Been a while."

"Oh!" Mom says. "Yes it has. Well, life happens! It does!"

"Janie," Dad says close in to Mom's ear. "Honey. Take it down a notch."

Reggie covers his mouth. I'm pretty sure he's laughing.

A FEW DAYS LATER I HAVE ANOTHER DREAM.

JASMINE IS AIRBORNE.

We are dropping together, whizzing through the air, but I am not afraid. Her flower wings wrap around me so I smell their light musk, so I feel her biceps clenched against my back. Our noses are so close they're almost pressed together. Her lips move. I still can't hear her.

But when I wake up, I know what she said.

Meet me.

I SPEND DAYS
ANALYZING THE DREAM.

After much perseverating I conclude the only way to meet her in midair, if that's even what she meant, is to jump out of a plane. At the very same time, I decide that I have truly lost my bananas.

At first, even though I really want to talk about it, I avoid the subject whenever I see Joe. We take walks, we mess around with plants, we hang out with his parents, we sell flowers, we visit Jasmine, we steam up windows. The dream persists. It gets stronger and louder. There are black flowers everywhere, all the time. Finally, I can't distract myself from it anymore.

On Saturday morning, I call Joe.

The conversation goes like this:

Me: Uh . . . hello?

Joe (sounding sleepy): Hi.

Me: Do you want to go jump out of a plane?

Joe:

Me:

Joe:

Me: Joe?

Joe (sounding less sleepy): Okay.

Me: Okay?

Joe: Yeah, okay.

Me: Oh.

Joe: Let me make a phone call. Meet me at my house in an hour.

Me (sounding panicked): Oh. Now?!

Joe: Now. Okay, bye.

Me: Okay. Bye.

Me (to myself): What have I done?

I'm almost positive this isn't what Marlene was going for when she told me to take life action on a practical level, but I take the bus up to Warrenton, drink some coffee with Norma and Bill, who now treat me like I'm a welcome addition to their current kitchen layout, and then we go.

It's on the way there, in Joe's truck, bouncing along, that I start thinking.

I'm not stable.

My body isn't ready for this.

What if the chute doesn't open?

246

Well, Eden, if it doesn't open, you will spatter like a bloody pancake. The good news is it's pretty great where you'd be going, so don't sweat it.

Joe is almost chipper, apparently free of dark thought, bundled in jacket, hat, gloves, a bounce in his usually measured demeanor. He's practically excited.

"Don't worry," he says. "We've got perfect weather. And if you're having second thoughts . . . I mean, are you sure you can do this? You checked with Spock, right?"

No I did not.

"I'm not having second thoughts." I cross my arms and stare ahead.

As I watch New Jersey pass by, I think how since I woke up, but really since Joe, my days are long, lifetimes long. Maybe it's because new things are happening instead of how my days used to be; waking, school, dance, sleep. Lather. Rinse. Repeat.

I scoot closer to him, lean my head on his shoulder. It's easy to touch him now, even though I haven't known him for long. But the thing itself hasn't gotten easier at all. Whatever it is that's growing inside me for Joe — it has teeth. It wants. To be closer, to kiss, to see the world through his eyes. It's not quite enough to be next to him, and I smart, knowing it's as close as I'll ever get. That's what I mean by teeth. I don't think anything will ever be enough, and this right now — that it's temporary and I can't hold on to it—the Joe-wanting monster in me gnashes against time and how it passes.

"You're sweet, Joe," I say.

It's funny how what comes out of our mouths only licks at what is true.

"You're sweet, too," he says.

248

JASMINE FINDS
ME IN MIDAIR.

It takes me totally by surprise. I was hoping, not expecting, but immediately she was there. About three seconds after we jump, as I'm trying to keep my guts inside my body and struggling to maintain my shit, my instructor vanishes, and Jasmine slams into my air space. Before I even know what I'm doing, I've latched myself onto her. Once her warmth is on me, it seems like she was always there, like she will always be with me, and I completely relax and sink into her. She is so strong, I get why Joe leaned on her. Even midair, she lends substance.

She's holds me and whispers in my ear.

Can you hear me? she says in the rushed whisper of a little girl. *Eden, do you hear?*

I blink and blink again. She's still there. I nod.

Why? I think. *How can I?*

We're in the air, she says. *It's neutral.*

I hug her, hug her so tight. *Jasmine, tell me what to do. Why won't you come back? Just open your eyes.*

She shakes her head.

Cami and Peanut, she says. *Tell Joe Cami and Peanut.*

I nod as the air whirs around us, deafening.

Now let go of me, she says.

I close my eyes and brace for pain, clutch her tighter. If she lets me go, I will fall and smash. There will be no waking up this time. I will go to the other place because there will be no more body here and nothing at all to come back to. Is that what I want?

It's not.

Joe is right behind me, falling too. I don't want to hit the ground and obliterate my body. Yes, it's a trap. Yes, it binds me to a gravity I would like to escape, most of the time. Yes, it's hard to be a person. It sometimes feels impossible to chop wood, to carry water.

But I don't want to die.

I want to live.

Jasmine is gone. My instructor points to the loop, and I remember. I pull.

And then, there's wind, cold, and I am flying. There is nothing yanking me up and nothing to drag me down.

This is the sound of silence.

250

Of seas parting, seeds sprouting, hearts breaking and mending, dancers snapping their hands and feet, stretching. Oceans rage against themselves, and mountains stand guard.

Like *kshhhhhhhh.*

Like peace.

Like an infinite exhale.

Shhhhhh.

This is between me and whatever mighty forces are at work.

I spread my arms wide to the sky, and I let go.

I am not afraid anymore.

When we land, I can't get the buckles and straps undone fast enough. I'm laughing and running for Joe. I hurl myself into him.

"Nice fall," he says. "Good job, Freckles."

Then I wrap my legs around him, my arms, my whole self, too.

"That was so —" he says.

But he doesn't have a chance to get the rest out because . . .

So many kisses.

I SHOULD TELL
JOE ABOUT JASMINE.

I know I should. I should have told him as soon as we landed, or maybe when we left the airport, or when we ate dinner after, or really any time up until now. But everything is so outstanding, and I know I can't explain to Joe how spectacular Jasmine was, how seeing her was a good thing. And what if I imagined it?

But I can't let it go. She gave me a message for Joe, and it has been on my mind, pirouetting on the tip of my tongue. I have been rehearsing what she said. *Cami and Peanut. Cami and Peanut.* Maybe I should tell him really fast and then get away from him so I don't have to watch the aftermath.

"I don't want to go home yet," I say, as we approach my house. I need to talk to him where we can be alone.

"Did I ever tell you you live in a fancy neighborhood, Freckles?" He smiles, his eyes combing the yards as we pass into the cul-de-sac.

He's been in a lighter mood than I've ever seen him since we jumped, like he was able to leave all his worries about Jasmine for the clouds to carry.

"Look at these houses." He downshifts. "What does your dad do again?"

"He's an architect. And my mom caters. She makes cakes and throws everyone's parties. Crazy Cakes. That's the name of her company."

"More people buying cakes than flowers," he says. "And houses, too."

"I guess."

I have never really looked at my neighborhood, but now I see it through his eyes. The houses are flawless. It's brown now because of winter, but in spring, all these lawns will be manicured to perfection, the dogs will all be groomed, the sidewalks pristine.

The sun is winding up to let loose an epic sunset. I have the right spot for us.

"Go up there," I say. "Follow that road."

"Here?"

I point him to the right.

"A cemetery?"

He pulls into the graveyard at the very top of Cherryville,

where Lucille and Dig and Reggie and everyone sometimes come to drink, and where I used to smoke when I was feeling morose and wanted to watch the whole town. There's no one here right now, though, like I knew there wouldn't be. Parker's having another party tonight. Everyone is otherwise occupied.

"Yeah," I say. "Seven generations of Joneses are buried here. Four generations of Cassidys. I have two sides of dead Irish relatives all over. I should feel at home here. Anyway, it's a good place to be quiet."

"That's because everyone's dead."

"Most dead people are better company than live ones." I open the door. "Want to go for a walk? I can show you where my family is. I could show you all their gravestones. They're right over there." I point to a patch a ways to the left. "The influenza years are a real drag. Lots of babies. But it's a good view. All the town lights and everything."

He steps around the truck to where I am. "You cold?" he says.

"A little."

The truth is I don't notice the weather all that much when I'm with Joe. Either that or it's actually milder weather since I met him. He's responsible for global warming. He puts his arms around me, shelters me in his big army jacket.

"We could dance." He sways some.

"Dance?"

He twirls me.

"Do you dance?" I say.

"This is about as much dancing as I can do," he says. "I don't think I'll ever be into clubbing if that's what you're asking. I don't think I could take the lights." He grins. "But I'd take you to prom and shake it some."

Prom. Another thing I thought I hated before that I can be excited about now. This boy on my arm for prom. Maybe my hair will be grown out by then. Maybe I'll be gorgeous. I know he will be.

Joe smiles shyly. "Can I see? I mean, will you show me?"

"Show you what?"

"You dancing." He stands back from me. "Show me."

"Here?" I have been getting better. I'm even starting to get a callus.

"Yes here," he says. "Show me what you're made of. Except — wait, can you?"

"Not like I used to, but yeah, I can."

And then I do a quick cabriole across the dirt in front of him. It's one of my favorite moves.

"What?" he says, grinning hard. "That's amazing. It's like you're hiding a superpower."

Joy comes over me, into me like a storm, like the river rushing, spinning me in silk again. My lungs are bigger and smaller and beat beat beat beat all up my legs and into my wrist bones and can't breathe and breathe in light, snow, pain, ballet, failure, jumping out of planes, holding hands, reaching under his shirt to touch.

He tightens and lifts my shirt too so our skin meets when he hugs me.

"Shouldn't have done that," I say.

And then we kiss, and I die and go back in time and reinvent what it means to kiss someone, to want someone's breath against yours, to shrink the days of your lives into this.

"Eden," Joe says, like a question.

My lips are numbing, tingly.

A flower blooms from his throat. I brush against it, and the In Between comes back to me.

The sun is all the way set now, and it's turning cold again, so we get back in his truck.

I want this to go on forever, him and me together, not worried about Jasmine, his smiles just for me, but it's not real. It's not dealing.

There's no more stalling. I have to ruin everything. Now.

"I have to tell you something," I say.

"You're secretly an astrophysicist?" He leans in like he's going to kiss me, but I push him away.

"No," I say. "I'm not an astrophysicist."

His smiles drops. "Oh crap, it's something major. What?" he says. "What is it?"

I kiss him, and it tastes salty even though no one is crying. I want to slur into him, so the lines between us are muddied, so we cannot be separated. I run a finger down his neck, his arm, then pull away so I can see him.

"I saw Jasmine again," I say. "When we jumped. She said something and I finally heard her."

"What?" His voice comes from far away.

"She had a message for you."

His hands are on my shoulders, and he's almost shaking me. "How could you not— Never mind, I don't even care. What did she say?"

"It might be nothing." I know the words are true only as I say them. "If it's nothing, I guess I am crazy. I don't want to be crazy. And if it is something, you might get upset."

We face each other. I am cold now.

"You might," I force, "not want me anymore."

"Tell me," he says.

The ground is suddenly slippery under our feet.

257

"It could be really, really important for you to tell me."

"It didn't make sense," I say. "What she said to me."

"Eden, please," he says.

"She said Cami and Peanut," I blurt out.

Joe sits all the way back against the window, and there is no color in his lips.

"Joe?" I say.

"You saw her." He wipes at his cheeks. "It was really her. Holy shit."

"Does it mean something? To you?"

"Her brother and sister. Peanut, Cami. They died in the fire that made her a foster kid. She always said she wanted to be with them when she was bummed out. We used to fight about it. I think that's why she always drove so fast. Idiot."

"Joe . . ."

The air has thickened so much in the truck cab that the windows are fogging. Snowflakes drop onto the windshield.

"I have to take you home," Joe says.

"I'm sorry I didn't tell you right away," I say. "I got scared."

He starts down the hill, not looking at me. Talking to himself, not to me.

"I should have been there for her this whole time," he says. "I should have been in the hospital all day every day so she would know she had to come back, not doing this."

This. He means me.

"I need to figure this out," he says. "About what to do with her. This whole thing is so fucked up."

"By whole thing," I say, pressing, "you mean me and you."

This is good, I want to say. *This is life. It's not selfish to live.* Digby and Lucille went on, and Mom and Dad did too. And they had the right to. Time served on planet earth is yours to use as you see fit. It keeps spinning, and just because someone's life ends or pauses doesn't mean we have to do the same.

"This one." I point down my road. "Make a left."

"I know," Joe says. "I've been to your house."

"That's right," I say. Seems like so long ago. Forever. "You brought flowers when I first got out of the hospital. I never said thank you."

"Yeah," he says. "You're welcome."

He pulls into the driveway.

"Tell me why you brought the flowers," I say, mostly because I don't want to get out of the truck, because once I do, I'm not sure I'll ever be here again, next to him.

"I ate the cake," he says. "The sour cream cake you told me to eat for her. I did and it made me feel better. I wanted to say thank you."

"Oh."

"That's what I told myself. Truth, though? You made me

forget all the bad stuff for a second. At the hospital. My mom. Jaz. I forgot it all talking to you. I got greedy. Wanted more of that." His eyes are shiny. "And plus you looked like you needed some flowers."

Joe is disappearing in front of me.

"Fate," I say, trying to hold him to me. "Destiny."

He's shrinking me into obscurity. "Just something nice."

When I can see that there's no use, that there's nothing I can do to bring Joe back to me, I open the door.

"That's it, hunh?" I say. "Over?"

He sighs like I'm a burden, like my question is absurd, but he quakes on the exhale. "Eden, I need to think. Alone. I have so much to figure out, and I can't do it mixed up in this crazy."

Crazy. He said it. And I guess I am.

"Eden, did she say anything else?" he says, as I wilt out the door. "Anything at all? Now's the time to tell me, okay?"

"Yeah," I say, and I can barely get the words out. "She said 'now let go of me.'"

260

DIGBY HAS HIS HEADPHONES ON.

*He's working on homework or some-*thing at the kitchen table. His laptop snaps shut, and he pulls them off when he sees me. The beats are still audible until he turns off the music. I'm shaking, and it's not like I can hide anything from Digby, but I try anyway.

"Why are you here?" I say, putting on my best cranky twin voice. Maybe the cranky will keep him away from my heart. "Aren't you neglecting your husbandly duties or something?"

He taps on the table. My tactic didn't work. He's about to dig into me, I can tell by the parentheses around his mouth. I want to confess everything, really I do. And it's not like I haven't practiced saying the words out loud. That's why I know without a doubt that there is no way to speak the truth, my truth anyway, without sounding bat-shit loopy. Not even to my brother. Maybe especially to my brother. You would think our twinness would make a difference. But he's a boy. He's still a boy who wants to fix everything. He can't fix me.

"Edes," he says.

I pull out leftover soup. "Want some?" I ask him.

He considers me while I beam nonprying thoughts at him.

"Totally," he says, finally. "Mom's white bean is the best."

"Mom's everything is the best," I say. "Toast?"

I get the thick-sliced sourdough bread down from the cupboard, grateful to be able to use my hands to do a simple task like making something to eat. Toast. I still cannot believe I went all those years without eating it. The crunch, the sweetness of the butter, the yeasty tang.

"You can eat that now?" Digby asks.

"I'm working on it," I say. "I'm okay with having to take it slow. It forces me to taste everything. And most of the time I've been able to swallow as long as I chew really well."

"Then yes, toast, and butter," he says.

"Okay." I pop the bread in and wait. "Where is she?"

"Mom? She got a call a little bit ago. Something went wrong at the Carson event, and she blazed out of here. Dad's already asleep."

"And Lucille?"

"Fred's." Her restaurant job.

"Right," I say. Lucille in latex, serving up burritos, equals good money but not much time off.

I pour us each a hot bowl of soup while Digby butters the bread. I hand him a spoon.

I haven't eaten since breakfast, and I was so nervous then I could barely get my oatmeal down.

Digby dips his toast, watching me as I chew each bite twenty times.

"Why aren't you at Park's?" I say. "Isn't he having a thing tonight?"

"I stayed behind," he says. "Wanted to make sure you were okay. I knew you weren't going to go."

"I'd go!" I say. It's the first time the idea of a party, of a bunch of almost not kids drinking beer and playing pool doesn't make me feel like knocking myself unconscious. It actually sounds kind of fun. "You want me to?" My lip starts to vibrate, and the back of my throat aches. Crap.

"What? Of course! I want you to come." He looks down. "I want me and Lucille to be in addition to you and me, not instead of. We're twins. We shared a uterus, Edes. And you know, I don't want to do anything except make sure Lucille understands that I'm not going anywhere."

"Unlike everyone else in her life," I say. "Including me."

"It's okay," he says. "I know something big happened to you. But it's the first time I can't reach you, that I don't know what's going on with you, who you are, what you want, what you're capable of, what you're into. I'm trying to get used to it."

"I saw you guys," I say. "When I was In Between."

He stops eating.

"What, like, when you were under?"

I nod.

"Bullshit," he says.

"You say you don't know what's going on with me and then, when I try to tell you, you say it's bullshit. This is why I keep my mouth shut. It's better that way."

"Okay," he says. "So tell me. I promise I'll listen."

And now that the door between us has cracked open, I don't know why it's been so hard to talk about with him. He will accept me no matter what. He's the other half of me. "You were in my bed." I chase the statement with a spoonful of soup.

It takes me a few seconds to look up, and it's like something I've been holding on to for so long rushes out of me. Digby knows exactly what I'm talking about.

"You were in my bed." I repeat it with more confidence. "You were with Lucille. You had your arm around her waist, and all I could see for the longest time was your hair making a sunset on the pillow." I sip on water. "You guys were cute."

His face is careful, watching me for signs of real insanity.

"There was Tylenol by the bed. You were in a red T-shirt.

Lucille was in some sweatshirt of mine. You had your arm across her stomach."

"Okay, okay!" he says. "I believe you!"

"I saw Mom, too," I say. "She was crying in her room. It was like I blinked and thought myself there. I felt like she knew I was with her."

"Lucille did too," Digby says. "She told me. That's why she was sure you were going to come back. She said you were smiling."

"I don't remember smiling," I say.

Digby sits back and crosses his arms. "Well, that's cool as hell," he says.

"What is?"

"Now we don't have to wonder. About what happens after we die. That's cool."

Like Spock said. I guess it is pretty cool.

"There are still things to wonder about," I say. "I didn't get very far."

"Doesn't matter," he says. "There's something. Not dead in a box like Mom and Dad always said."

"There's something," I say. "But there are different rules than people think. So I don't know—I still feel like there's no time to waste."

"You're going to stay, right?" Digby says.

265

"Stay?"

"Yeah," he says. "Don't leave me here on this lonely planet. I'm a twin. I want to stay that way."

"Me too," I say, but when I try to reach for him, he scoops the bowls out from under us.

He rinses our dishes for a long time.

Outside, it's black.

"You want to run?" I say. "We could run to Parker's."

We used to run together all the time. Him for basketball, me for ballet endurance, for long, thin limbs.

"Or we could drive," he says.

"I can do it," I say. I show him my sad little biceps. "I am strong." I think about Joe, Jasmine, the hospital. "Come on, it's only like two miles."

"Okay," he says, doing a few hamstring stretches. "I guess we can run over there." He grins at me. "But I'm not going to slow my pace for you."

I smile. "Sure you are," I say.

PARKER'S HOUSE IS MAYHEM.

Literally every senior at South High is here, and I'm pleased to see someone is puking in Parker's mom's bushes, so that part of the experience is complete. The music is loud, but not so loud the cops will come, and the house is filled with pot smoke and empty red plastic cups. Parker is nervously manning the keg in the corner.

Life has returned to itself.

"Red, get over here and sit down with your old friend!" Reggie yells from the couch.

"I'm going to get a beverage," Digby says. "Want one?"

"Nah," I say. "I have to get up early."

"You're sweaty, and you smell," Reggie says, when I park myself next to him.

"Why, thank you," I say. "As I like it."

Reggie searches my face. "Why are you jolly?" he says.

I look around. I like these people. I don't hate them anymore, and I'm not afraid. Those are all things to be jolly about.

"I don't know," I say. "I'm feeling better."

"Nuh-uh," he says. "Don't tell Reggie lies."

"No really! I'm dancing again."

Maggie Blathorn falls across our laps, and we roll her off, watch her fall to the floor, laughing.

"She's gonna pee her pants," Reggie says. Then he sniffs me.

"What?" I say. "You already told me I smell."

"Yeah," he says. "Like lust." He sniffs again. "Like *love!*" He hoots with laughter. "Oh my God, you're in love. You're in love." He singsongs. "Those lips have been kissed by someone who actually likes it. Where is he? She? Where? Where?"

"What the hell is wrong with you?" I say. "Shut up."

"Mm-hm." He leans back, satisfied. "That's what I thought."

Digby stands next to us, a cup of beer in hand. "What are we talking about?"

"Nothing," I say. "Maggie peeing."

Because I am not in love. I can't be. With someone who doesn't want me? It's too complicated. Too messy. Too everything.

From Almost Dead: True Stories of the Afterlife

It was just your standard, run-of-the-mill heart attack. Too much ice cream and the like. Too much stress, most of all. Happened right in the middle of the classroom, a couple days before I was retiring. You know, unless you have a document stating otherwise, paramedics will revive you if they can. Even if it takes thirty-seven minutes, like it did for me. Even if you might wake up a vegetable, which thank goodness, I did not.

Do I remember anything? You bet I do.

I saw my body as they tried to revive me, all the kids hovering around, then I felt this . . . well I can only describe it as love. Also acceptance. I was sure I could put my arms around all the hurt in the world and fix it with all that love, that's how much I had, how big it felt. Can't get back to that now. That feeling.

I also saw a woman. I didn't know her. She wasn't from my past or my family or anything. She was made of light, and when she hugged me, it was the best I've ever felt. She might have been an angel. I don't know.

Thirty-seven minutes is a long time, turns out. But then I came back. And here I am.

— *Vera Geldoff, 70, retired teacher*

INSOMNIA SUCKS.

I couldn't sleep at all, imagining Joe and what he must be feeling or thinking, about me, about Jasmine. At three in the morning it seemed perfectly clear that Joe was not someone I wanted to let float out of my life and disappear, that there was more to us than comas and Jasmine, that whatever happened to her, he and I were at the beginning not the end, and I had to find out what would happen next. I even composed a vow, while mooning out the window, half drunk. Scrawled it on a piece of paper.

To you, I pledge my sword, my word, my fealty. I will stand in front of trains and leap to take the bullet, battle shadows and demons for you. When you need me to, I will fold around you, an ocean that will lull the pain from you. I'm sorry about your friend. I'm sorry about how we met. I promise we'll get past it. I promise I will be the best of myself.

In the light of a sort of hungover day, I'm not sure of anything except that my insomniac writing is super dramatic, but I decide to stick to my plan, to go to the hospital, to find Joe, to declare myself, to stand at his side no matter what comes. Because that's life. We have to choose something.

My head hurts from the couple of watery beers I had last night, so I shower the blur off and then start harassing Digby for a ride. The buses don't run on Sunday, and I need to get to Warrenton. I don't have PT or therapy today, but it doesn't take much for me to convince Lucille and him to take me up there. I don't really have a plan, only that I'll find Joe and we'll figure this out together.

Of course *us* has been hard for him. No one planned to have this thing happen.

So we head to Warrenton, Digby and Lucille and Wren and I. My mouth dries out, and evil dragon creatures beat me up from the inside, but other than that, it's a regular drive along a pretty highway on a nice day.

"I'll be right back," I say, when we get to the parking lot. I'm hoping I'll find Joe and we can go somewhere to talk. Then these guys can go home.

"Knock 'em dead, kid," Wren says as I close Beast's door.

I don't bother with the elevator. I am already picturing myself in Joe's arms, remembering the feel of his skin against my own, reminding myself not to squeeze him too tightly when I get to him.

And then I'm standing at the window to Jasmine's room

271

and it is empty. There is no Joe. There is no Jasmine. The bed has been stripped, the curtains are pulled back and slung over a chair. The flowers are gone. The bedside table is clear. There are no machines. Nothing is slithering, nothing is beeping. Nothing.

"Is she awake?" I shout down the hall. "Is Jasmine awake?"

I already know. You don't wake up and hop out of bed, get released within a matter of hours. That's not how it works. I know it's over with Joe, too. He'll never be able to look at me without thinking of his dead best friend, without thinking it was somehow my fault.

I rest my head against the glass.

"No," I say.

"Hey," Sally says, and lays a hand on my back.

"Hi," I say. "She's gone?"

"Sorry," she says. "She passed yesterday."

I slide down onto the floor, let my legs splay out in front of me. Sally adjusts her scrubs and wedges herself next to me. This is because of me. Did Joe come here, crazy from what I told him last night, and have her unplugged?

"Her organs started shutting down yesterday afternoon, one by one. She held on until Joseph got here last night and then she left about ten minutes later. Rita said it was peaceful.

It's a blessing, she did it herself. I don't think that boy was ever going to be able to. He would never have let her go."

I goose up, hard, like Jasmine is next to me, breathing on my neck.

"I can't believe I wasn't here," I say.

For Joe. He had to be here alone.

"Oh, hon," Sally says. "She was already gone. If she had woken up at this point, she would have been half a person. From everything I've heard about her, she wouldn't have wanted that."

"Still," I say.

"I know it's tough when anyone dies." She pats me. "What was it with the two of you?" she says. "You didn't know her, did you?"

"No," I say. "And yes."

How can I ever explain the connection we made? I can't and I won't.

"I don't feel good," I say.

"Course you don't," says Sally. "It's not the way anyone would have hoped this would turn out." She rubs my back. "Okay," she says. "Okay."

I wonder where Jasmine is right now. What comes after In Between?

Between life and death. Between awake and asleep. Between

in like and in love. Between black flowers and white ones. Then what?

"She wasn't going to come back," Sally says. "I knew it when she came in. Some patients are determined, and you can feel it."

"Even when they're in a coma?"

"Even then. Some make moves. They twitch. They open their eyes. They show signs that tell us not to shut them down. You can't base everything on that, of course. You can't make choices about whether a person breathes or not based on intuition. But you get one anyway," she says. "An intuition, I mean. And I'm telling you, I knew she wasn't coming back the second they brought her in here." She chucks me under my chin. "Just like I knew you would."

"Yeah?" I say. "Doesn't that make you sad?"

"No," she says. "Why should it? We all have our path to walk. And you brought fire in here with you."

"Hellfire," I say.

"Life fire." She uses my knee as leverage to get herself up to standing so she peers down at me like an overlord. "You won't have much of a reason to come around here anymore," she says.

"I will," I say. "I could never go too long without seeing you guys. I wouldn't get to hear about Jake."

"Rhonda's pregnant," she says. "That's all she wrote. Nothing else to know."

"I would miss you," I say.

"Well, you shouldn't," she says. "I have too much work to do to have you hanging around here. I know Spock feels the same. Rita, too." Her voice quivers. "We'd all appreciate it if you kept your distance from here on out."

"That is not nice." I stand.

Sally turns up her nose. "Nice is overrated."

"Bye, then," I say.

"Bye," she says.

I hug her. "I know you love me," I say into her shirt.

"Beside the point," she says. "You are an awful distraction."

"Yeah," I say, "you too. Better off without you."

"Better off," she says. "That's right."

In the lobby, Norma hands me a carnation. I can see Beast in the parking lot, feel my phone vibrating.

"I was going to tell you when you came in," she says. "About Jaz. But then you sped on by and I didn't get the chance."

"Thank you," I'm trying not to fall to the floor weeping. It is not my turn to weep. "For the flower. It's really pretty."

"The funeral is Saturday," she says. "A small gathering at the restaurant. She's already being cremated." She sighs. "I don't know why Joe didn't tell you about Jaz."

"Yeah," I say.

Cremated that fast. Poof. Like that. No more body.

275

"The gathering is at one," she says. "You could come."

I see Joe how he was last night. I know how much pain he must be in right now. He said he needed to figure himself out without me. And what if he pushed me away? What if he told me to leave? I couldn't stand it. I would combust.

"I can't," I say. "But thank you."

"He'll be cleaning out her room at Gigi's after. In case you want to be there. For Joe," she says.

"I don't think he wants to see me, Norma," I say. My throat is so inflated I can barely speak.

She twirls a lily, watching me.

"Did you know, I met Joe when he was five?" she says. "When his mom first got sick, his dad and him, they used to come into the shop to buy flowers. My mom and me, we thought he was the cutest thing. Gigi, too. We all fell in love with that boy."

Joe. My Joe, I think. I'm jealous of everyone who has ever gotten to be close to him.

"He was a lone wolf, that's what Gigi would say. Said she could see his spirit animal walking alongside him."

What's mine, I wonder? Something that gets eaten by wolves, apparently.

"We introduced Joe to Jasmine after his mom passed. The

276

two of them, her so hurting from the fire." She peeks at me. "You know about the fire?"

"Yes," I say.

"They were two peas in a pod," she says. "From then on. And then there was you. You're the only other friend he's ever brought home, and something about you has scrubbed the tarnish right off of him. Don't give up on him," she says. "You two look good together."

"Yeah," I say.

If there was a pane of glass between Madame and me, this is a brick wall. This is the Great Wall of China.

"I'll see you soon," she says.

As I get close to Beast, Lucille jumps down.

"You okay?" she says. "You run your errand?"

"Yeah," I say. "We can go home now."

IT'S TIME TO DEAL WITH THE SHRINE.

Outside, the sky is clear, and this morning I am clear, too, about the things I need to do so my life makes sense again.

The day starts in the dark, with Madame, sweating, muscles burning. At the barre, stretching until my ligaments scream, running warm-ups until I'm in tears.

Still, that satisfaction, though. After, not during. The only thing that keeps me from thinking about Joe. More pain.

And now school.

I haven't gone anywhere near my own locker since I've been back, and I caught a glimpse of it covered in pictures on my first day. It made me feel like a ghost, like I was dead and patrolling the school hallways and didn't know it. So all this time I've been hauling my books around the school, doing anything I can to avoid having to look at myself plastered and suspended on metal.

But now I feel different about that shrine, like those pictures have me trapped in a Before when it is time to have an After.

A.C. After Coma. I like it.

Back to beginnings and endings, the list:

- I never heard from Joe yesterday, though I waited and waited. Ending.
- *Peter Pan* was an ending too. The end of me feeling sorry for myself.
- Jumping out of a plane, dancing in a graveyard, going to a party. Beginning. Beginning. Beginning.
- Back to basics with Madame. Beginning. And an ending. The end of lethargic Eden, crazy Eden, not-really-alive Eden.

By now I know no one is going to touch this locker but me. No one would dare. I get it. They're trying to be nice or respectful or something. I march up to it. There are pictures of me dancing, my school picture from last year when I had bangs, articles about the accident from the paper, pictures of me and Digby, me and Lucille, all taped to my locker. They're worn at the edges, peeling, showing their frailty and age.

"Happy Monday, sister," Reggie says, coming up behind me, our entire posse with him. He leans against Lucille's locker and watches the people as they walk by. "I don't think I'm going to miss this place when it's all over."

"We're starting to look like suspicious grownups hanging out in the elementary playground," I say, as a couple of freshmen pass us.

"No doubt," Reggie says. "I can't wait for a summer of nobody telling me what to do, where to go. Graduation!" he says. "It's coming."

"Sad though, right?" Parker says. "We're all going our separate ways."

"Oh, hell no," I say. "We are not doing this now. We still have months to get through. We're not there yet. Save this speech for June."

But I feel it now, anyway.

"Why are you staring at your locker like that?" Parker says.

"I don't know," I say. "Guess I'm trying to figure out how I feel about this thing."

"There was a lot more stuff at first," Lucille says. "People were even lighting candles, which is a total fire hazard. It was nuts."

Lucille munches on an apple and leans her head into Digby's shoulder. "The school took some of it down when you woke up," she says. "But they left this, I guess so you wouldn't think people had forgotten about you or something."

Reggie hulking all over the place, Parker looking like Parker. Lucille and Digby looking like Lugby or Ducille, whichever you like better. For better or for worse, my people.

I dig a nail under one of the pictures and pull the whole thing down in a single motion and turn back to my friends.

Reggie puts his arm around me. "That's right," he says. "You do you. Have I told you how glad I am you made it?" Reggie says. "For real, Red. Gave me heebedies when you were dead, like you were going to sit up, jerk around, crawl off the bed, and suck my soul out of my mouth." He vibrates air between his teeth, then opens his mouth wide and flails zombie arms about.

"You wish," I say as the bell rings.

"See you at lunch," Digby says to Lucille.

"Yes," she says. "The only way out of the fire is through it. I shall fear no Elaine. I'll see you at lunch."

He kisses her for about ten seconds longer than what's proper. I have to look all the way away, because Joe.

"Edes." Lucille folds her arm into mine as I shove the old pictures into the nearest trash can. "You okay?"

Lucille bites at her bottom lip where she does so often her mouth is a deeper red with a permanent indentation.

281

I want to say, *I almost died and then I got mixed up with a dead girl and fell in love with a live boy, and now the world feels strange.*

"I'm fine," I say.

Patient name: Eden Jones

Patient has made significant progress. She is taking interest in her schoolwork and her dance, and seems to have an improved outlook on life. She has opened up considerably. Continued therapy is recommended, but not compulsory.

MY MOTHER IS IN BED.

She is napping because she's been working overtime to make mocha mousse cakes and chocolate-dipped strawberries, heart-shaped cookies and sea salt truffles, and to invent specially curated valentine menus for the upcoming holiday.

She is in the exact position she was in when I was In Between, lying on top of her covers, in a sweater and jeans, her face smothered in pillows. She isn't crying, though, and I am not a ghost.

I get into bed with her, careful not to disturb her, and take in her warmth, her merino sweater.

"Hi, honey." She strokes my arm, half asleep, turns on the pillow so we're facing each other.

I look into the fine lines and softening skin.

"Hi, Mama."

"You need something, sweetheart?" she says. "A shake?"

"No," I say. "I don't have those anymore."

283

"Right," she says, barely awake. "Yay."

"I wanted to be close to you," I say.

"Oh," she says, "I love that."

"Mom," I say.

"Mmmm?"

"I think my heart is broken."

She opens her arms to me, and I snuggle in. "Baby," she says. "Tell me everything."

I shake my head. I can't. Joe is a deep cut, no stitches, not healed, still digging to the bone.

So Mom holds me even tighter. "I'm here," she says. "Whatever you need."

"It's a privilege to have a mom like you," I whisper, almost inaudibly. *"You are the best one."*

Mom squeezes but doesn't say a word.

I drift into sleep holding on to her like I used to when I was little.

When I wake, she's gone and a fluffy white blanket is draped across over my shoulders, tucked in tight along both sides of my body so I am safe and snug.

Snug as a bug in a rug.

IT'S A HELL OF A DAY FOR A FUNERAL FOR A LEATHER JACKET.

The leather jacket I wore when I had my accident, to be exact. Lucille decided it would be healthy for me to say an official goodbye to the me from before, and once she had the idea that it was all connected to the jacket I always used to wear, Wren jumped on it and then I had to allow it, because it became more of a craft-slash-cooking project than anything having to do with me.

They say a snowstorm is coming, but today it feels like spring, not winter.

Not too far away, a real funeral is taking place, for a real girl.

But here we're playing pretend, and I am trying to convince myself that this is the best and only way, and that Joe wouldn't want me there anyway. It has been a trying week. I can't get myself to believe he will be happier without me, but he will definitely be less tied down. I keep thinking about how there are certain people you can't get rid of, no matter how hard you try, and then there are people you're held to by the thinnest cord and all you have to do is snip. Your lives will be disconnected. You will never have to see them again. Your life will go on as though that person never existed. But then you have to go on with a cord dangling from your chest. And what happens to their piece of the cord? What happens to their piece of you?

Maybe it's not as simple as a single snip.

After this day, Joe can go back to being the guy who's going to travel the world with one bag, who doesn't even believe in being with another person seriously. He can be free.

Me, I don't know how long it will take me to get over him and how green my life became with him. From where I'm standing, I'm going to go with forever.

But life goes on, right? *Time and tide wait for no man* and all that.

So we're in the backyard getting ready. Everyone is coming. My parents, Digby, Parker, and Reggie. Madame, Benita, and even Marlene are coming. Marlene is molting she's so excited.

Do it for them.

"I really don't understand your choice of outfits," Lucille says to Wren. "You should demonstrate a little consideration for the occasion. It's like you're not taking this seriously."

Wren, who is wearing her favorite glittery jeans and a neon

286

green long-sleeved shirt, scoffs. "It's not a real funeral," she says. "We're burying a jacket." She says it slowly, with careful enunciation. "Nobody died."

"Nobody died," Lucille repeats, then looks at me. "Kinda."

Lucille is covered in dirt from digging up a corner of the yard, sporting paint-spattered overalls.

"You're right, Wrenny," I say. "This is stupid. Can't we just have a BBQ instead? Pretend it really is spring? And don't pick on her," I say to Lucille. "Look what you're wearing. You're not exactly fancy."

"Um," she says, "are you forgetting about my very impressive English-royalty-type hat?" She taps on her black old-lady cloche with the flowery veil. "I resent the implication that I am not taking this seriously."

"In actual fact, I'm the only one who's appropriately dressed," I say.

"Now, see?" Lucille leans on her shovel. "That is totally unfair. You have goth tendencies and didn't even have to change clothes."

Wren painted my nails black and silver last night in preparation. I am participating.

For some reason, Lucille has dug a hole big enough to bury a horse. She's determined and after a vigorous handwashing, has now moved from that task to setting the picnic table for the post-burial feast.

"Do you want a box for the jacket?" Digby says, rounding the corner. "Or do you want it as is?"

"We'll lay it in the dirt," I say. "Return it to the earth."

"Put it in the box," Wren says. "It'll be like a coffin."

"Morbid much?" Lucille says.

"Okay, if you don't want it to be morbid, why are you having a funeral in the first place. Anyway, I could paint it for you," Wren says. "Put some sequins on it or something."

"Just when I think you might be growing up on us," I say.

"I am growing up," she says, "but I will always like sequins and glitter."

"I would love to let you paint the box and go all out with your glitter, but I don't think I have time."

"Why not?"

"Because everyone will be here soon," I say. "But go get some markers. I hear coloring is super soothing."

"Here you go." Digby hands us some markers. "Lucille wants to make a banner, so all the stuff is out." He sighs. "My lady she loves banners."

Wren gets the empty box, and we draw.

"Here it is." Mom has what's left of my leather in hand.

It's a crinkled, shrunken raisin.

* * *

Mom called in to school on our thirteenth birthday. She lied to Barb, the school secretary and ruler of all things middle school. She told her Digby and I had both come down with what she was certain was nothing but a pesky twenty-four-hour flu. We were floored that she would break a rule. And lie to Barb. Barb could have your ass in a second if she wanted to. We had never seen Mom do something like that.

Then we climbed onto a train and she took Digby and me into New York for the day. Dad had a big presentation, and things were hard for him during the recession, so this was a huge deal. We didn't hold it against him that he couldn't be there. We were used to it being the three of us anyway, and I think we all felt the same way: free.

We went to lunch at an Italian place. I ate chicken, and Digby ate pounded, seared liver. After, we sat on a bench and watched the models go by, killing time till the Broadway show we were going to see that afternoon.

That's when I saw it, in the window of a secondhand shop on Christopher Street in the Village. I was as drawn to it as if it were a person curling its finger, beckoning me to it. When I wrapped it around myself, I felt like me, for the first time ever.

That was the day I decided New York was going to be my

boyfriend, and nothing would distract me. I would be faithful and be rewarded for that faithfulness. Someday I would live there. It was where I would be famous and have an apartment and live the dream. I know. Lots of people have that dream. It's not new or original, but it was mine, and it became possible the instant I pulled that jacket over my shoulders and zipped up that zipper.

Looking up didn't seem so scary then.

✻   ✻   ✻

"Yes, though I walk through the valley of the shadow of death, I will fear no evil: for you are with me; your rod and your staff they comfort me," Lucille says, then pauses and whispers, "Well, go on."

"How did you learn that?" I say.

"Google," she whispers again.

I can't help but be a little self-conscious. Madame and Benita, Parker, Reggie, Lucille, Digby, Wren, my parents, Marlene, everyone standing around this pile of dirt. For what?

"Edes," Digby says, and even though I know this whole thing is pretty monumentally stupid, Digby has to hold me by the wrist and shake it so the colorful box falls into the ground, into its hole, to the place where drowned jackets go to die.

Lucille hands me a mason jar with some dirt in it.

"Do it," she says.

But I can't, and I don't know why. I start laughing. It's not a gentle laugh, either. It's a long, loud, ugly one. I want Joe. I want to lean on him, to feel the wool of his army jacket scratch my cheek.

It's not because I'm lonely. I don't mind being alone, I swear I don't. It's because he's like my stupid dead jacket, except he's alive and bright and so real it hurts to have him being all those things away from me. Covered by him, I feel most me.

"It's okay," Lucille says.

I sink to my butt, the hysterical laughter turned to hysterical tears. The harder I try to control it, the less I can. I put my palm up to shoo them away as they all come closer like we're going into a football huddle. They all say my name. *Eden, Edes, Red.* No one calls me Freckles, and that's all I want to hear. Where have the flowers gone? Where is my magic?

I want to flee into the house. I need a panic room, somewhere to hide until everything makes sense. Just when I thought my life was going back to the way it was supposed to be, I have discovered that I don't want it that way anymore.

To everyone's credit, they're mostly quiet while I sit there and lose it. Then, when my breathing is normal again, Lucille rests her hands on my shoulders like she does, and then it's me and her, alone in my mother's garden, in my garden, and she looks at me with the kindest eyes.

"This isn't a joke funeral," she says. "This jacket *was* you."

"Fine." I shake her off of me, take a deep breath. "I'm fine."

I stand up and talk to the dirt.

"Dear Leather," I say, as sternly as I can muster. "You served me well, and you will be missed. May you bring smiles and protection to the dirt and your awesome trusty leather afterlife, as you did to me."

I tip the jar over the box.

"Nice one," Digby says, and scoops some earth off the pile next to the hole. "My turn."

I KNOW IT'S RUDE TO ABANDON YOUR OWN FUNERAL.

But I have to. I need to be alone.

I need to go to the river.

As everyone is munching on burgers and potato salad, I sneak out of the house and march down the hill. I'm going back to my spot, where I hurt myself, where I haven't been since I woke up.

I turn down Union Street, away from all the people walking their dogs. Women chat, sip cups of coffee. It's so freaking quaint. I want to get away from it, want the water now.

I take one deep breath at Bellamy, more air than my lungs can manage, then hit the towpath, crunch on the dirty snow where the towpath never gets sun, leave town behind. In the summer, there will be families on bikes, moms running strollers, dogs everywhere, but no one is out here now. It's as quiet as a deserted planet, not even a wind or the flutter of a bird.

The rock stops me. Where I bashed myself.

If I stand here long enough, the piece of me that never left this place, the piece I can't get back will stroll out of the bushes like a hologram, oblivious to what is coming. When Lucille gets here and cries over my brother, that part of me will comfort her, best I can. I'll be trying not to be afraid of the life that will unfold for both of us now. I'll try to convince her to control herself, use her head. We'll drink some tequila. I'll stand, stretch myself high, try to shake off my melancholy, then . . .

Fear.

I trip. My skull thuds against my rock. I realize my mistake, inhale, lose consciousness, float on my back among sheets of ice. Lucille runs into water, almost drowns herself, pulls me out. I watch her scream, her blond hair matted against her cheek. She pumps at my chest. She runs.

I survive.

I survived.

This is not only the place where I hurt myself. It's more than that. I stumbled on it with Mom and Digby when we were six and Mom was having quality-time guilt because she'd been trying to start her business and hadn't been hanging out with us enough.

This meant lots of wandering around together, because what else do you do with a couple of kids who never want to leave home? Digby thought the abandoned train car was scary, and he held my hand like he did when he was stressed out, with his knuckles jammed into mine so I had to feel his discomfort. He didn't want to get in the water, even though it was so scorching humid, because the river scared him, that sound it made.

Not me. I was smitten.

These willows. Mine. Water dribbles down the rocks, and I am hypnotized. Everything falls away, drips from my feet and sinks to the bottom of the river like sediment. I stand on my rock, close my eyes, throw my hands into the air, offer myself up. This time I don't fall. Roots rip through my feet and crush the stone beneath.

An owl hoots in daylight.

And then she's here. Jasmine. Still in her dirty white tank and jean shorts. I don't move.

"What are you afraid of?" she says.

"You," I say. "Are you real?"

She kicks at leaves. "Real as the dead get."

"You going to miss it?" I say.

"I should ask you the same," she says, and shakes her head. "I love my boy, you know."

"Joe." Saying his name brings the pain, head to toe.

"You have to decide." She rubs her bald head. "Make a decision about what you want. Like that poem about the two roads and the choosing and stuff."

"Robert Frost?"

"Yeah!" She brightens and claps her hands together. She seems more alive than humans. "Decide and decide again. But you decide on Joe, you stay. He doesn't need a flake."

This nails me. Joe could be with me. That's what she's saying.

"And if you mess with him, I'm going to give you a haunting you'll never get over," she says. "I'm talking mad poltergeist shit, not sheets with holes for eyes. I will terrify you."

I run my hand over her shoulders. She's soft as petals.

"Still wondering if I'm real?" she says.

"Jasmine," I say, "why can you talk to me here, after all the other places?"

"You know why," she says. "We touched."

Like this.

We hold each other's hands.

Irises: green and brown and blue

Pupils: shrinking and growing madly

Eyelashes: translucent, nonexistent

Eyelids: thin

Sclera: almost disappeared

Breathe, we say, and flowers bloom from our lips.

And then she's gone.

JASMINE'S ROOM.

Joe is on his knees among boxes. A few days of tribulation have left him leaner, hungry-looking.

All around us are pictures. Pictures of black flowers. I never knew knees could actually buckle, but now mine do, and I sink to the floor.

"Oh my God," I say.

"You missed the funeral," he says. He folds a blanket. "I thought you might show. There were only a couple people there. Gigi even went. Not you, though."

"You didn't call or text. After what you said, I didn't think you wanted me there."

"I didn't have the juice to ask." He rubs his eyes. "It's been a long week."

"Yeah, it has." I look around. "You want to hear something crazy?"

"Why not?" he says.

"I've been seeing these flowers everywhere since I woke up.

You remember how I wouldn't tell you what I was seeing? It was these. And they're real. At least in here. You can see them, right?"

He touches the pictures. "These?" He comes over and sits next to me. "Jasmine's favorite. They grow in winter. She thought they were romantic. Said they meant love and toughness and bravery. I should grow some of these. Especially now."

"I'm sorry, Joe," I say. "For not being here for you."

Joe puts his arm around me, then kisses me easy and sweet, like I've been missing, each touch the slow shaping of a lathe, remaking me.

"Lots of things are bad," I say, when we pull apart and I'm faced with Joe's bruised-looking eyes.

"They are," he says.

"And life is dangerous. The world is dangerous."

"It is," he says, hands on my waist.

"But so many things are good, too."

Joe runs his lips over mine like he's handling something new and precious.

"Joe," I say, "I know you said Jasmine was your one great thing—"

"I didn't mean—"

"No," I say, "I know. I . . . but you're mine. You're my one great thing. My best thing. Okay?"

We both breathe faster. My heart thumps in my ears, my throat.

"Yeah," he says. "Okay."

Then I roll him over, and we make out for roughly nine hours.

We do not fall off a cliff.

An ocean of black, satiny flowers surrounds us.

They sway behind him.

WHEN I DIE, IT WON'T BE THE EARTH I'LL MISS, ITS FLORA AND FAUNA, ITS TAIL FEATHERS AND POMP, ITS SEASONS.

It won't be combat boots or leather jackets or perfect buildings. It won't be dressesTVspillowcasesriversmountainscomputerssmartphonesfashionpotteryevenmusicevendancingevencloudsintheafternoononlazydaysnotevennoteventhesun. It won't even be the sun, or the stars, or that warrior supermoon. It will be the people, the animals, the alive things that touch. And not their bodies, but what's inside, the glow.

I don't care what you say.

That there is no soul, that it's all made up.

Maybe you're right.

But, no you're not. You're wrong. I know it.

What I mean is, we aren't our stories. I'm not a privileged girl from suburbia, or a dancing prodigy, or a dancing failure.

I'm not a smart girl or a dumb girl or a girl who likes to wear leather and lace. And Joe isn't a victim, he isn't a sad boy who lost his mom or his best friend. He isn't even a florist, and he's definitely not a prince or a knight on a white horse. We do have to rescue ourselves in the end, no matter how much we learn to lean on other people. We aren't here to save each other. We will never be anything but flawed and subject to change. We aren't one thing. We aren't even two. We're a thousand. We're a million. We're facets. Starshine.

What's behind the stories, or under it, that's what I'll miss.

Still, I'm sitting here in a room of black flowers with Joe, and we are both real and alive and that is something.

And doesn't that mean that whether there's an afterlife or a soul or a soul mate or a benevolent or angry god, whether there's magic or sorcery or nothing but stark pain, whether there's reincarnation or however many virgins waiting in heaven — doesn't that mean I have to live?

Rilke said to *have patience with everything that remains unsolved in your heart, to* live *the question.* I can do that. I think I can do that now.

"Joe?" He's lying next to me, our hands touching.

"Yeah?"

"Nothing, I was just making sure you're real. You're real, right?"

301

"Real as an alive person gets," he says.

There are a lot of ways to die. But for now, I choose life.

Patient name: Eden Jones

Glasgow Coma Scale Test

Eye Opening Response: Spontaneous (4)

Best Verbal Response: Oriented to time, place, and person (5)

Best Motor Response: Obeys commands (6)

Total score: 15

Prognosis: Optimal (best response)

AFTER

Found handwritten in the back of *Almost Dead: True Stories of the Afterlife*

I hit my head. I was hanging out with my best friend, and it was icy. I was upset about unimportant things, not paying attention. Then I drowned, and it was like my life flashed in front of my eyes, sort of, except it was more like I went into my past. I saw some strange things, and then when I woke up, a month had gone. It took me a long time to feel like I was all the way back. For a while I felt like I wasn't anyplace.

To tell you the truth, the scariest part of it isn't what happened; it's what would have happened if it hadn't.

If I hadn't had my accident, I wouldn't have the life I do; I wouldn't know the things I do, either. Everything would be different. I would be oblivious. So yes, I guess I do believe in fate, and I believe that was mine, at least the beginning of it. Sometimes I like to put quotes on my ceiling, things that remind me who I am or who I want to be. I hope I'll always do that because it's a good way to remember important things. Right now it's

307

this from the poem by Charles Bukowski called "The Laughing Heart."
I think it explains what I'm trying to say better than I can. At least I hope
it does. I hope it helps you understand exactly what I mean. Because life
is hard and people are crazy and they hurt each other and suck so much of
the time. Life is mysterious and scary and frustrating. But it's also beautiful and bright and magical. It's also yours. So own it. I mean, why not?

> your life is your life.
> know it while you have it.
> you are marvelous
> the gods wait to delight
> in you.

—Eden Austen Jones, 18, dancer

ACKNOWLEDGMENTS

Many thanks first to my HMH family: Mary Wilcox and Betsy Groban, whom I am privileged to have worked with; Lisa DeSarro, Amanda Acevedo, Ann Dye, Rachel Wasdyke, and everyone else who has provided support, pep talks, and championed my work; my copy editor, Ana Deboo; and the talented designers. Most especially thank you to my super-deluxe editor, Elizabeth Bewley. I would hang out with you any day, for any reason. I love your brain. You're the radness.

To the incomparably brilliant Martine Leavitt: Once again, without your support, this novel literally would not exist. Like, at all. So thank you for words both kind and stern, and mostly for saying "You can."

And, of course, to my agent, Emily van Beek: I am so spectacularly blessed to have you standing in my corner. You are fierce, graceful, and creative beyond measure. I have a million loves for you.

Thanks to Molly Jaffa at Folio, who is a master of all things foreign, and also to everyone else at Folio Literary Management. I do so enjoy having the Justice League in charge of my career.

To all the foreign publishers who have been so wonderful, and to all the readers, librarians, and booksellers I've been lucky enough to meet, or write to, or interact with: You're the best. I know everyone says you're the reason for the writing, and it's true. You are.

I owe a huge debt of gratitude to the brilliant ballerina Camille Cooper, who interrupted finals week multiple times to answer my cries for help; to Dr. Mary Seiler for setting me straight on comas; and to my dear Sunny Moore for her green thumb. Also, to the many people who sent me emails and drank coffees with me and explained to me what it felt like to almost die: I know it wasn't easy, and I thank you for trusting me.

To Laine Overley and my brother, Chris Eagleton, who take my kids without question when I have to leave: I could not do any of what I do without you, and I am so grateful.

To the Taos mamas (you know who you are): You're like a swarm of really loving but edgy butterflies that hold me up, and I thank you.

To Stuart, my sweet friend: You are strong and will prevail.

Thanks to my son, Bodhi, who likes to write his own stories by my side, and who always asks me how it's going with the books, and to my daughter, Lilu, whose singing, laughter, and moxie light up every day — UR mom!

To Chris, you're a freaking starshine miracle. I can't even believe all the support, plus your hand in mine. I'm stunned by my great fortune every single day. Like, what?

Last, this was written in the wake of loss. First, Cinnamon Martinez, who loved suede boots and fast cars and had such a killer smile; Javon Orion, who, like Jasmine, never stopped moving until she did. And, finally, to my friend of twenty-five years, who was both one of my greatest loves and most difficult lessons, Tanya Feher: You did not wake up. I am startled every day by your absence. I hope you are all safe and free and somewhere floating on flowers.